MW00852518

LOST IN THE DARK

Dark Sons Motorcycle Club - Book Two

ANN JENSEN

Published by Blushing Books
An Imprint of
ABCD Graphics and Design, Inc.
A Virginia Corporation
977 Seminole Trail #233
Charlottesville, VA 22901

©2021
All rights reserved.

No part of the book may be reproduced or transmitted in any form or by any means, electronic or mechanical, including photocopying, recording, or by any information storage and retrieval system, without permission in writing from the publisher. The trademark Blushing Books is pending in the US Patent and Trademark Office.

Ann Jensen
Lost in the Dark

eBook ISBN: 978-1-64563-901-5
Print ISBN: 978-1-64563-902-2
v1

Cover Art by ABCD Graphics & Design
This book contains fantasy themes appropriate for mature readers only.
Nothing in this book should be interpreted as Blushing Books' or
the author's advocating any non-consensual sexual activity.

Acknowledgments

Thank you for reading Book 2 in my Dark Sons Series! I love writing about these sexy and protective men and their Brotherhood. I'm going to admit that on some level this all still feels like a dream to me. Who knows, maybe by book 7 the reality of it will finally sink in?

First and always, I want to thank my family who is a source of never-ending support and love. Without their understanding none of this would have been possible. Mike, as always, you are my sounding board and weekly sanity check. I'd like to thank Kristin and Cam whose laughter and love made me smile when my real life was crazy. Someday you need to tell me those stories you swear will inspire new novels. Avery, girl I know you don't like me saying it but you saved my life, thank you!

A big thanks to Stephanie who was my primary Beta/Crit/Developmental partner. You helped me through the roughest version of this book and helped make it awesome. Thank you Katie for being an awesome book coach and helping me focus and find my niche. To all the beta readers who looked this book over you are amazing. Whether you gave me one or one hundred comments I appreciated each and every one of them.

To the amazing team at Blushing Books thank you for all your support and wonderful advice. Sandra, your encouragement and kick butt edits are amazing! Patty, your cover design has everyone I show it to drooling. Also, Ruth, the promo images you came up with are awesome.

Finally the biggest thanks goes out to you my readers, because none of this dream would be happening if you didn't want to read my work. I would love to hear from you. Find me at:

Webpage: https://www.annjensenwrites.com
Twitter: @annjensenbooks
Instagram: annjensenbooks
Facebook: https://www.facebook.com/annjensenbooks
Email: AnnJensenWrites@gmail.com

Chapter 1

Don't confuse my personality and my attitude because my personality is me and my attitude depends on you.

Two years ago

The icy sweet and salty flavor of her margarita, and the smokin' hot eye candy around the bar, were the only things keeping Tari from ditching the shallow women seated next to her.

Agreeing to go out with her roommate had been a mistake. The two of them had established early in the semester that they had little in common. Her roommate was a cheerleader whereas she enjoyed the quiet Zen of Yoga. Tari loved small gatherings while her roommate went for big parties. But Tari hadn't known how to politely refuse the invitation to join her roommate and some of the cheerleading squad in an end of semester celebration.

After two hours and three dive bars, the effort to keep her mouth shut was starting to make her jaw ache. Tari prayed the shallow women would forget about her when they stumbled off to the next one. If Jamie, the leader of said cheerleaders, spewed one more snobby or bitchy thing, Tari was going to find her own way home.

This whole night was just one more in a long list of failed social experiments. It was like the women didn't even notice how vapid they sounded. She didn't belong with the cookie cutter trust fund babies and it was obvious with just a glance. With dark amber skin from her birth mother and pin straight ebony hair probably from her unknown father, there was no hiding that Tari's ancestors did not hail from the European continent. Her clothes were nice but not a single piece contained a designer label, and she couldn't have cared less. She worked hard for both her money and her scholarship and wasn't in the least bit ashamed.

Tari didn't go out often so her social experiences were limited, but she was fairly sure these women would be considered rude by any decent person. The bitter taste of resentment burned at the back of her tongue because she was all too used to rude. She had been 'saved from savagery' by the Christian missionaries who adopted her. With them, she had traveled to a new country every year only settling down a few years ago in a religious commune. She lived everyday surrounded by a toxic mix of piety and superiority. The only reason they were allowing her to go to college was because they assumed she was going to school to become a missionary doctor to further spread the word. Superiority because of money, background, or religion was complete nonsense in Tari's mind.

She just had to survive tonight then two more years of school. Tari hid her smile behind her glass focusing instead on the hum of the happy bar crowd surrounding her. The last two bars had been crammed full of college kids with the same top hits playing repeatedly. The stink of bodies blowing off steam with abandon had made her slightly ill. However, at this bar, rock music was a fun background to the lively conversations. The people around them had an edge that reminded Tari more of a jungle then the tamed, bland animals in a zoo. Most of the men wore leather vests and clothes of hard-core bikers while brightly colored women strutted in oh so skimpy outfits that drew the eye. Tari wished she could spend hours studying the unique and surprisingly fit people around her, but the crap going on at her own table made that impossible.

"Twenty dollars says I can get the hot gardener at the bar to buy me a drink." Jamie smirked and tugged down her top to expose white surgically enhanced cleavage.

The flinch that hit Tari caused her to spill a bit of her drink. Denver wasn't exactly the United Nations and this bar wasn't any different, so it was all too easy to guess who the twit was talking about. A gorgeous man, standing at the bar, with warm golden skin leaning forward and talking to some friends. His dusky skin tone, sharp features, and straight black hair made her think he had Native American or South American heritage. She would have to hear him speak to be sure of which it was. However, Tari was more interested in the fact his muscles were a perfect example of the male physique. The worn black t-shirt and jeans he wore hid nothing and had her imagination questioning if he had the illusive V that melted any woman's panties.

"You're going to hit on someone from here?" Her roommate whisper-shouted sounding shocked.

Jamie waved her hand dismissively. "It's not like I would bring him home to my parents... geeze. You act like you've never taken the help for a ride."

"And I'm done." Tari threw back the last of her drink. "It's been interesting meeting you all but I'm going to call it a night."

Tari stood feeling a little tipsy, but for once enjoyed the fact she towered over the petty bitches. At 5'11" she usually avoided heels, but Tari had wanted to dress up tonight and her kick ass leather boots had three-inch heels allowing her to tower over them.

"You can't leave yet," her roommate whined. "We haven't gotten to ask you to join the team!"

Tari grabbed her purse from the back of the chair. "What team?"

"Cheerleading of course." Jamie said it like Tari had just asked the stupidest question in the world. "You're tall, strong and supposedly flexible since you do that yoga stuff every day. You would be a perfect spotter."

Tari didn't even know what a spotter was. What had given any of these women the idea she might want to be a cheerleader?

The token brunette of their crowd cleared it up with her next statement. "We couldn't get any more guys to sign up. You're built like a man so close enough. Plus, since you are a scholarship student you have to have good grades and we need the boost."

All the girls nodded. What the hell did grades have to do with cheering? And did the idiot think calling her manly was a compliment? Alcohol fuzzed her brain, but she didn't think that even sober she could follow that logic.

"Let me get this straight. You want me to be your manly charity cheerleader?"

"No need to shout." Her roommate pouted.

"You have got to be kidding me." Tari wanted to throw drinks on all the little Barbie doll wannabes and ruin their perfect makeup.

"I thought you said she didn't have an attitude?" Jamie asked with confusion contorting her face.

"Attitude?" Tari spoke ten languages fluently but when she got really mad she fell back on the Spanish she had spoken most of her teenage years. "E*res tan patético, que resultas entrañable tu hija de una hiena.*"

Ignoring the stunned looks, Tari grabbed her purse, deciding to settle her tab at the bar and get the hell out of this place. She would worry about making friends another time. Pulling out a twenty from her wallet she headed away from the pack of women.

Jamie was out of her seat and grabbing Tari's arm before she made it ten steps. "Did you just call me pathetic, you low class piece of trash?"

Tari looked down at the woman, who barely came up to her chin, saying nothing because she didn't trust the anger boiling inside of her.

Tari noticed the bar had gone silent though the peroxide blonde had not, and continued her rant. Jamie huffed and flipped her overly stiff hair. "You're the pathetic one who couldn't even see we were just pitying the poor charity case, who wouldn't even be in college if her freaky ass cult didn't pay her way."

Tari ripped her arm out of the bimbo's grip. "*Meapilas.* If it wasn't for your daddy's purse strings and an overpaid plastic surgeon, you wouldn't even be on your precious Cheer team."

The gorgeous example of human anatomy at the bar burst out laughing, and his deep, gorgeous voice sent chills down Tari's spine. Jamie flicked her hair over her shoulder glaring at the man. "What are you laughing at Jose?"

Tari didn't know if the shiver that ran up her spine was from rage or the terrifying look that formed on the man's face. She couldn't believe Jamie wasn't running away from that glare because she would have been if it were focused on her.

"You should leave." The chill in the man's voice felt like it dropped the temperature in the bar by a few degrees.

"You can't tell me what to do," Jamie huffed.

"No, but I can," The burly bartender replied. "I reserve the right not to serve entitled little bitches."

"You'll regret this. I'll tell everyone what a shithole this place is."

The bartender laughed. "God, please do. I can't stand when you spoiled college kids ruin a good place."

Jamie seemed to notice she was the center of everyone's attention. It was impressive the amount of looks she was getting with a mix of disgust and outright hate. Tari took a little bit of pleasure in watching the bimbo brigade scramble to leave. Her roommate didn't even have the backbone to glance her way. When they were out the door the whole atmosphere swung back to normal and everyone started talking again.

Not wanting to risk bumping into the women outside, Tari made her way to the bar figuring one more drink then she would call for an Uber. Facing her roommate wouldn't be fun, but it was only two more days till she headed home for winter break and maybe she could get a dorm change before she came back. For right now, she was just going to see if maybe she could get another smile out of the gorgeous man at the bar.

Chapter 2

When opportunity knocks, grab that bitch and take her for a ride.

Dragon studied the Amazonian goddess who was making her way to the bar. Practically painted on jeans showed very muscular thighs and the sweetest round ass he could imagine. Her simple red cotton shirt was technically modest but tight enough that he could follow the curves of her bra as it cupped her breasts. The boots she had on made her over six foot tall but that was simply perfect for him. At 6'6" he enjoyed not feeling like he would crush a woman.

Her hair reminded him of ebony waves of water that, along with the shape of her eyes, spoke of a mix of Asian and African genetics. Who was this woman who spoke English like a Midwesterner and threw Spanish insults like his mamma?

Dragon moved over a bit and gestured for the mystery woman to join him. When she was close enough, he could smell a hint of vanilla. "Can I buy you a drink?"

He wasn't expecting the burst of almost musical laughter his comment incited. "I'm sorry. I don't mean to laugh. I would love a drink."

Colt, owner of the bar Dark Times and tonight's bartender, walked over giving the new woman a friendly smile. "I'm Colt and the dour man standing next to you is Dragon." The grizzly bartender winked making the woman smile. "Your drinks are on the house if you can tell me what you said earlier to make this usually stoic lump laugh."

Dragon didn't think he was that bad. He just didn't skim through life joking. Between being a SEAL, prospecting for the Dark Sons, and taking care of his mom and sister he didn't often have time for fun.

"Cool names, mine's Nefertari, but my friends call me Tari." She got an adorably embarrassed look on her face. "It wasn't really that funny, my temper gets the best of me sometimes. Basically, I said she was so pathetic it was cute, and she was a daughter of a hyena, and then I called her a hypocrite. See nothing special."

Dragon shook his head. "That may be what you meant to say. My mama says a *Meapilas* is a bible thumping *gringo* who preaches fire and damnation but would piss in the baptismal font if it was more convenient."

"Good to know," Tari muttered.

Colt burst out laughing more at her obvious embarrassment, than at the joke. "Beer and a margarita coming right up."

Dragon couldn't help but reach out and push the gorgeous woman's hair away from her face. "How did you end up with those–"

"Bitches?" Tari leaned into his touch a bit. "One of them was my roommate. I'm hoping to get a switch before next semester."

Dragon ran his thumb over her cheek before letting his hand drop. "What are you studying?"

"Pre-Med right now."

"Going to be a doctor? Impressive."

"That's what my parents think." He watched her take a sip of her drink with a bit of amusement.

"Not your plan?"

Dragon enjoyed the sight of her chest rising and falling as she took a deep breath. "I've been dragged around the world with them my whole life. Missionary work is their life. Having their adoptive daughter working alongside them as a doctor is their dream."

"But not yours?"

"Not even a little. My plan is to become a physical therapist. Help people through the pain and back into their lives. I want to make them stronger in who they are, and not try to change them into something I think they should be."

The passion he saw lighting up her face somehow made her even more beautiful. She was like a banked fire just waiting to flare up and he wanted to feel that heat against his soul. The more they talked, the more he wished there was some hope of taking things further. She was like a breath of fresh air after being stuck in an underground cave for weeks.

"That is a good goal. Your parents wouldn't approve?"

"Not even a little bit. They want someone to obey not to think." She took a sip from her margarita and waved her hand as if dismissing the conversation. "What do you do for a living?"

Dragon hadn't been drinking as much knowing he had to get up at the crack of dawn. "I'm in the Navy."

"Really? You don't look like military with the long hair. Do they let you grow it long because of your perfect muscles?" She winked at him teasingly.

Dragon winced hoping Colt hadn't overheard that particular statement, but that hope was useless.

Colt laughed "You are sitting with a bonafide SEAL and an undercover party boy."

Dragon loved the sparkle of humor that lit her eyes like candlelight.

"I can totally see that." She smiled at his friend before turning back to face him. "Are you stationed here in Denver?"

"No, I'm on leave. My family lives here. I go back tomorrow."

It made him feel good to see her shoulders droop slightly in what he hoped was disappointment. "I guess that means dinner tomorrow is off the table."

Dragon was surprised he felt a tightening in his chest at the thought of not seeing this beauty again. The two of them had been flirting, nothing more, but the connection he felt with this woman was incredible. "Unfortunately, yes. I'm just staying in town tonight to be close for my transport. I don't know when I'll be back, it could be months."

Or with how dangerous his job was it could be never. His enlistment was up in seven months and he still wasn't sure what he planned on doing.

"Closing time," Colt shouted to the half empty bar.

Was it really two o'clock? Dragon couldn't believe how quickly time had passed.

"Give me your phone." Tari held out her hand. Amused, Dragon unlocked the screen and handed it over.

She navigated to his contacts and entered in her information. "In case you decide you want to catch up next time you're here."

Dragon smiled and thought he might just do that. "Let me give you a ride home, *Querida.*"

Chapter 3

When life throws you a curve... take it!

Tari had never ridden on the back of a motorcycle before and the experience was exhilarating. Feeling the play of his stomach muscles under her hands while she was pressed up against him, with the vibrating motor between her legs was almost enough to trigger a mini orgasm. When they stopped at a light, the alcohol in her system gave her the courage to explore lower, and what she found had her heart racing.

He was large and hard, pressing, what had to be uncomfortably, against his jeans. She stroked along the edge and found the tip of him poking slightly out of the top of his jeans so all that was between her hand and his dick was the thin cotton of his shirt.

"You're playing with fire, *mamacita*," he growled.

"I know, *Papi*." The endearment felt naughty as she said it.

But it felt right. "How long do you have before you have to leave?"

"Three hours is all I can give you, *Mami*." The sexy Spanish nickname had her thighs clenching. His voice was harsh as she used her fingers to tease his length.

"I'll take it." Her breath rushed out of her as he took off heading a slightly different direction now ignoring the posted speed limits. Ten minutes later they were parked in front of a motel and he was lifting her from the bike.

Tari wasn't used to being manhandled like a child and found she loved it. Their mouths clashed and it was like a war of pleasure each one trying to memorize the other's tongue. Her back slammed against the door forcing them both to come up for air.

"You sure about this, *Mami*? The only promise I can make is, if I take you inside, I'm going to make you come so many times you'll be screaming my name."

Tari only had one sexual experience before with a long-term boyfriend and it had been nothing like the pure need she felt at that moment. She had never had a one-night stand and, being honest with herself, this would probably be one. Even knowing that, she would never forgive herself if she didn't give in.

"I'm sure."

He opened the door behind her and she almost fell backwards into the small room but caught herself and walked backward till the edge of the bed touched her legs. Like every motel, there was barely room to walk, the majority of the space dedicated to the King-sized bed. By the entrance, a green satchel was propped up ready to go. A door at the back of the room probably led to a bathroom and a small dresser held an ancient TV. It was surprisingly clean looking for a roadside motel. All thoughts about the room fled, when Dragon closed the door with a click and pulled off his t-shirt in a single, swift motion that Tari had only seen in the movies.

Every muscle stood out in brilliant relief, including that perfect V that led down into his pants. Tari wasn't sure if she should applaud or begin worshipping. Gorgeous, colorful dragon tattoos wrapped around his chest like ancient warriors. Tari had the urge to lick every line.

"I love the way your eyes sparkle like the night sky. Reminds me of the stories of Citlali: goddess of the stars."

He bent down to untie his combat boots and Tari wanted to catch up. She unzipped the sides of her own boots toeing them off. She was very happy she was wearing a pair of her sexier underwear; tiny red boy shorts that she decided to reveal by turning around and pulling her jeans slowly down her legs ending in a perfect *Uttanasana* yoga pose leaving her bent perfectly in half looking at Dragon upside down from her ankles.

He stood unmoving, his pants unzipped and hanging just off his hips. She could see lust sparking in his eyes as he took in her seductive pose. Spreading her legs a little to give him a better view, she pulled off her shirt leaving her bent over in nothing but red underwear and bra.

"You're flexible." His voice was a growl that shot right to her core.

"Yoga classes almost every day. I also have excellent balance and muscle control."

She had never talked like this or even considered herself a sexy woman, but something about this man had all her darkest fantasies bubbling to the surface. She was absolutely naughty as she dropped her hands to the ground and slowly moved into crow position, then into a handstand.

"*Cristo*, I can see how wet you are for me."

She was about to drop her feet down when Dragon was there pulling her panties up and off her legs. She almost lost her balance when he bent over and ran his tongue up her thigh teasing along the edges of her pussy.

"Dragon, as much as I want your lips on me. I can't hold this position when you do that."

He stepped back letting her lower her feet but as soon as she started to stand, she was tossed onto the bed like she weighed nothing more than a throw pillow rather than the 168 lbs. she knew she weighed. Blood rushed out of her head and before she got her bearings, he was spreading her thighs, his tongue finding her core like he was laser guided.

A loud moan was all she could manage as he teased with his tongue, coming close to, but not ever touching her clit. Pleasure built and almost exploded, as he eased first one finger then another inside her. She had never had an orgasm brought about by someone else, but there was no doubt in her mind, tonight would change that.

"You taste so fucking good, *Mami*. I could spend all night tasting you."

"Please, Dragon, *Papi. Te necesito!*" She was so close if he would just do something more she knew she could fall over that edge.

He did something with his fingers stroking a spot deep inside her, and his lips latched around her clit, sucking hard, causing lights to explode behind her eyes as the biggest orgasm of her life obliterated her senses. She screamed out her pleasure and all of the overwhelming feelings that needed somewhere to go.

"*Cristo*, you are so beautiful." Dragon kissed his way slowly up her body, slowing to let him draw each nipple into his mouth, starting the fire of desire building back in her core. When his mouth reached her's, Tari tasted herself mixed with his own unique flavor.

His kiss claimed her in ways she didn't even know she wanted to be claimed. This man, at this moment, owned every part of her heart and soul. It didn't matter he was going away to do dangerous things. He would always own the part of her soul she was giving him right now.

His hard length slid back and forth against her core in time to their kiss and, without a second thought, she lifted to meet his next glide welcoming him into her depths. He was so big, she thought for a moment he wouldn't be able to fit all the way inside her. Letting out a breath she relaxed, letting her body accept him.

"God, you're so tight. Fuck, what are you doing?" His words were muttered against her lips as she used her Kegel muscles to pull him deeper inside her.

She had heard about the benefits for both parties, but this was the first time she had tried it out. If his moans were anything to go by, she was doing it right. He slowly pulled out on her next contraction and she felt the tip of his cock rub against that spot his fingers had found earlier, and she knew it wouldn't be long before she was thrashing in pleasure.

He worked his way in and out of her, so slowly and gently she felt like she might go crazy. She tried to thrust up to meet him and his hands pinned her hips to the mattress. He groaned so deep it sounded like a frustrated growl.

"You are so gorgeous, every thought and sensation echoes across your body."

"Watch my body echo later. Fuck me now."

"So demanding." He gave her several quick thrusts and she screamed, loving the feel of him, brutally pushing her closer to her goal of an orgasm that she knew would shatter her into pieces. But then he slowed back down and she growled her frustration. "What, *Mami*? Don't you like it slow and gentle?" He tilted his hips accentuating his words, dragging his cock along her G-spot causing shudders of tiny orgasms to roll through her body.

If he kept this up she knew she would go wild with need.

She arched up catching his lip in her teeth and biting gently down. "*No seas tan dulce. Cógeme duro, Papi.*"

"Fuck, I love your dirty mouth. You want me to fuck you hard, *Mami*?"

"Yes!"

Dragon grabbed her leg and hiked it up, as he slammed so deep inside her she thought he might break through to her uterus. Her scream of pleasure unhinged something inside both of them. They fucked like they were fighting: clashing and clawing at one another, overriding any thoughts until her whole body was a mass of nerves firing with explosive pleasure.

"Dragon!"

All her muscles tightened, spasming. His cry of release matched her own.

———

At five a.m. Dragon never regretted anything more than to have to walk away from the sated, sleeping beauty in his bed. Knowing it was probably wrong, but needing to capture the image forever, he snapped several pictures of her naked, sleeping tangled in the sheets. The note he left wasn't nearly enough but he would call her first chance he got.

Beautiful Tari,

I would have woken you but the sight of you lying there was too precious to interrupt. The mission I'm going on will have me out of communication for several months. I know we made no promises but when I call, your gorgeous voice will be the answer to a sailor's prayers. Think of me often.

Hasta mas tarde,

D

Chapter 4

Sleep is like a unicorn. It's rumored to exist, but I doubt I'll see any.

Ten weeks after the hotel

Standing in front of the Naval recruitment center her hands clutched in front of her, Tari wasn't sure what to feel.

Kicked out and shunned by her parents and the community she had grown up in. Then left at the bus stop on the edge of town with only a backpack of clothing and her wallet had been mortifying.

All because the close-minded hypocrites thought her pregnancy tainted her. The fact the father was military and not one of the fellowship made the whole thing unforgivable even if she had been willing to pretend repentance. The little bit of money she'd saved from her job as a yoga instructor had been barely enough to get her back to Denver and rent a tiny room in one of the worst parts of the city. Thank goodness, her job had health insurance and the clinic she had gone to had given her and her growing baby a clean bill of health.

Tari stepped inside the office knowing this was her last hope of finding Dragon. She had tried to remember the name of the bar where they had met but she couldn't even remember what part of the city it had been in. Nerves and probably the baby had acid burning at that back of her throat.

"How may I help you?" an older man dressed in a smart Navy uniform asked. His name plate read CPO Melker.

"I'm trying to find a way to contact a Navy SEAL."

His smile was friendly giving her hope he wouldn't laugh in her face. "Any particular one?"

"Sorry, yes." Tari fidgeted. "His name is Dragon. I met him while he was on leave in Denver two months ago."

"I'm assuming Dragon is his callsign. Do you have his real name? Rank? Where he is stationed?"

She felt stupid. Why hadn't she considered Dragon wouldn't be his real name. The bartender had said something about his station but she, for the life of her, couldn't remember. Here she was knocked up and she knew little to nothing about him. "No."

"Are you sure he was really a SEAL?" She saw the man's gentle eyes flick down at her hand unconsciously rubbing her stomach and she thought she saw pity in their depths. This was it, she was going to be going through this alone.

"This was a bad idea. I'm sorry I bothered you."

"No bother. If you get any of that information don't hesitate to come back."

Tari hurried out. Her last hope of contacting the father of her baby, crushed.

———

Seven months later

. . .

Tari took deep breaths trying to find her center. Exhaustion and strained muscles had her on the edge of tears. When she had dreamed of becoming a mother never had she thought she would be giving birth in a run-down bathtub of a studio apartment with no company. At least the midwife was willing to work for a couple hundred dollars. Warm water sloshed, as she tried to find a slightly more comfortable position. Her body shook with the beginning of another contraction.

"We're almost there, Tari. It's time to push." The midwife's voice was calm, helping her focus.

Deep breath in. Pain rocked through her as she bore down with the contraction. Tari tried not to scream but she must not have been successful as her neighbors once again pounded on the wall. None of that mattered though; it felt as if her body was tearing in two.

"I can feel the head, Tari, you are doing great."

She didn't feel like she was doing great. She felt like a complete failure. No father for her child. Living in one of the worst neighborhoods in Denver. Giving birth in her studio apartment bathroom because her job put her on leave during her later months of pregnancy and she couldn't afford a hospital. The contraction eased up and Tari felt tears pouring down her face.

"We're almost there. Just one more contraction should do it and you will get to meet your child."

Her child. Girl or boy didn't matter. She would be an amazing mother. Her child would never go a single day without knowing they were loved and wanted. She might not be able to provide luxuries, but Tari would find a way to make sure her child was healthy and happy.

"Here it comes. Push, Tari!"

She clenched her jaw and screamed, not caring what anyone thought. She roared her determination and promise to the universe and pushed. The whole world went white for a moment then the pain was just gone. Small splashing sounds had Tari opening her eyes to see the midwife pulling the most beautiful baby up and out of the water. The squall of life echoed in the small room as the woman used a small suction bulb to clean out her baby's mouth.

"It's a girl."

Tari reached out her arms and took her tiny daughter into their first embrace. Her cries died down as warmth seemed to pass between them. Tiny hands and feet, skin lighter and a touch more amber than her own with a fuzz of ebony hair. Dark eyes twinkled even in the low light of the room. Perfect. She was absolutely exquisite. How Tari wished she could share this moment of perfection with a family she didn't have.

"What are you going to call her?"

She looked down into her daughter's almost black sparkling eyes and heard Dragon's voice echoing in her mind. "Her name is Citlali. For the stars in her eyes."

Chapter 5

*Every day I arrive at work with good intentions and a great attitude…
then idiots happen.*

Present Day

Tari struggled to get off the bus with her daughter on one shoulder and the diaper bag and stroller in her other hand. She knew her boss wasn't going to be happy that she was bringing her child to the evening class but what choice did she have? Her now ex-babysitter had answered the door drunk off her ass. Now Tari was going to have to find another sitter for evenings who was willing to take the pitiful amount she could afford to pay.

The truth was if it weren't for the health benefits, she would have quit a long time ago. Being a yoga instructor at Dark Zen wasn't what she had dreamed. The makeover the owners had done two years ago had given her hope that the place was going legitimate, but the last few months had her feeling less comfortable every day. A wellness spa in an area of Denver that bridged the line between the poor and middle class could go either way. Unfortunately, it became harder every day to ignore the side businesses going on in the back rooms. What really concerned her was the age of the recent 'masseuses'. Just last week, when she had tried to talk to one of the girls, she had been taken to task for making customers uncomfortable.

Apparently speaking anything but English was forbidden, and since the Ukrainian girl didn't speak more than a few words of English it made conversation impossible. Mario and Fifi, the studio managers, were jerks on an epic scale caring only about lining their pockets and what the paying customers thought. She might be willing to look the other way on a lot to make sure she had insurance for her daughter, but the line was quickly approaching for what she was willing to accept.

The owner, Dozer, was a mystery and only talked about in whispers, but if she ever met the illusive man she would definitely let him know her thoughts on a few things. Once on the sidewalk, she got Citlali strapped in and rushed down the several blocks to the studio. Luckily, her daughter seemed in a good mood today so maybe her bosses wouldn't even notice her.

She only had one class tonight, but it was one of her favorites because of the students. The activewear rich crowd mostly stuck to the classes run by the completely unqualified, but hot, men the managers cycled through.

She rushed through the lobby and into her studio dropping her stuff in the corner.

"Well isn't she as cute as a June bug in July!" Val, Tari's most eccentric and, by far, favorite student, exclaimed. Val reminded her of a country singer: all big red hair, sparkly clothes, and over the top personality.

Her very southern compliment was followed by the laughter of Pixie, one of the newer members of the studio. "That pink flower headband is just adorable. Can I hold her?"

22

Pixie was just what her name implied, tiny. At five foot one the blonde woman was so delicate Tari sometimes wondered how she didn't blow away in a stiff breeze.

"Sure." Tari couldn't help her proud mama smile. "But be careful she likes to grab at shiny objects."

Pixie always wore a silver choker, that had a pendant dangling from it, even when exercising. The two women cooed and bounced her sweet girl while Tari laid out the mats for all the regular students. The two women were always the first to arrive and with their help the music was set up and the room ready by the time the other students arrived.

"I didn't know you had a child, Tari." Val's voice was wistful.

"She was the reason I was away those months last year."

"You didn't want to teach while you were pregnant?" Pixie asked while bouncing Citlali on her hip.

"Mario and Fifi thought it best; said a fat yoga instructor would lose customers." The loss of income and insurance had been why she had been forced to go with a home birth. Luckily, she had found a midwife and everything had turned out okay.

"They actually said that?" Val sounded horrified and it eased some of Tari's own anger.

"Yup."

"Pregnant is not fat." Pixie rubbed her own little baby bump. The woman was the size of a tiny doll but had the personality of a giant just like her friend Val.

"No, it's not. So why are we just now getting to meet this bundle of joy? You should have brought her in when you came back."

Tari loved these two ladies, who were becoming more friends than students, but they really didn't understand the realities of her world. "I'm technically not supposed to have her here now, but there was an incident with her usual sitter so

23

here we are. I'm hoping if I give her cheerios and juice, she'll sit quietly. She doesn't talk much yet, but when she does..." Her first words had been up and down when she wasn't even a year old. The little girl loved copying yoga poses even if it often led to humorous tumbling.

"Don't you worry none if she kicks up a fuss, I'll get her for you," Val volunteered.

"But you're paying for a class. You shouldn't have to—"

"I want to. Now get your overly bendy butt up to the front of class and let's get started."

The class went well and Citlali was well behaved, if a bit amusing as she cheered during a few of the more difficult positions and echoed her mommy every time she said the words *up* or *down*. Everything would have been fine if Fifi hadn't stuck her busybody nose in during the last five minutes, and seen Pixie blowing raspberries on the little girl's tummy during the child's pose. The woman knew at a glance the girl was Tari's since she was the only person in the class with skin darker than tan.

Tari waited for the blow-up as she dismissed everyone with smiles. Her students hadn't been bothered by her daughter being there and most gave the little girl a smile as she left. But Tari knew, from too much experience, she would probably be hunting for a new job tomorrow.

"Ms. Jones, see Marco and I in the office now." Fifi's whiny voice filled the room as Tari was putting away the last of the mats.

"I'll be right there." Tari pasted on a fake smile and did her best to find her inner Zen.

She walked over to take her daughter from Pixie but the woman waved her off. "We've got her. Go see what miss stick-up-her-butt wants."

Val nodded agreement and gave a pissed off look in the direction of the manager's office.

Tari set her shoulders, slipping on her sneakers to face the music. The manager's office held a fake version of every kitschy new age item one could buy. Tari hated the space. Instead of the true flow that should be in a place like this, it was more about marketing then relaxation.

She stepped inside and Marco's fake, hippy grin was instantly replaced by a sneer of disgust. Fifi stood in her designer suit smirking behind her husband, a vicious anticipation in her eyes. The married couple played upscale hippies for the customers but Tari knew white trash and that was what these two were.

"I received a complaint that you brought your illegitimate child into class today."

Tari bit down on the words she wanted to say and went with something more neutral. "From one of my students?" She tried to calm herself with a mantra of 'I need the insurance' but it wasn't helping.

"That doesn't matter. After the incident last week, I have no patience for your nonsense. We can't have our customers seeing our employees as anything but upstanding citizens. I was nice enough to let you come back to work here even after your lapse in morals last year."

Tari's temper won the battle over calm. "My lapse in morals? Are you kidding me? At least I don't use the massage therapy rooms as my personal bordello to fuck every hot customer and employee like some people around here." She looked right at Marco then snapped her gaze to Fifi. "My morals are strong enough that I don't sell prescription pain killers as healing supplements to pad my income like others. So please show me where in the employee handbook it outlines the moral code I've supposedly broken."

The door to the office opened and Val walked in, eyes blazing. Immediately, Marco and Fifi put on their professional masks though the tightness in their shoulders showed the anger they were planning on venting as soon as the customer was out of earshot.

"Mrs. Summers, we'll be right with you. I'm afraid we're in the middle of a personnel issue." Marco practically simpered at the woman. Tari could have warned him that sucking up wouldn't work on this southern belle.

"I would say this place is in dire need of some personnel changes. Starting with the two of you."

"Excuse me?" Fifi pulled herself up to her full height and looked down her nose at Val. "Just who do you think you are?"

"You're about to find out." She whipped her phone out of her bra and dialed a number putting it on speaker.

While the phone rang, Marco and Fifi looked baffled at each other. For once Tari had sympathy for the pair because she didn't know what was going on either. A deep voice answered the phone, "Hey princess, how was class today?"

"It was great, baby. You're on speaker, honey. Would you do me a favor and tell the two morons we have running Dark Zen they're fired?"

"If that's what you want they're gone." The deep voice chuckled.

"Who? Who is that?" Marco stuttered.

"Dozer Summers. Owner of this fine establishment. You two really never put it together? My lifetime membership and the free services to anyone I brought with me." Val rolled her eyes. "Definitely not the brightest bulbs."

"Am I going to have wrongful termination to worry about or do we have cause, Princess?" Dozer's voice didn't seem to be concerned either way.

"I'm guessing if you pull the feeds you'll find drugs and hanky-panky a plenty." Val smirked at the horrified expressions on the pair's faces.

"What feeds?" Fifi had true fear in her eyes now.

"The signs on every door that say this place is monitored

for your protection aren't just for show. My old man likes to make sure I'm safe and this place has enough hidden cameras to make a nun blush." Val seemed proud of the fact her husband spied on her.

"Or they can just leave nicely and we won't have to bring in the cops," Dozer's voice chimed in.

Marco was sputtering and Tari enjoyed every second of it. Fifi must have been the survivor of the pair because she said, "We'll leave."

Tari watched slack-jawed as the pair scurried to gather up their things and practically ran from the building. There must have been even more going on then she had thought to have the pair running away like Hell itself was chasing them.

"I'm stuck in Wyoming for the next two weeks, but I'll get someone over there to keep the lights on and start going over the books." Dozer's voice cut into the stunned silence.

"Understood. I miss you to bits." The real love in the woman's voice made Tari's heart ache wishing she had someone who loved her like that.

Chapter 6

When someone tells you to "Expect the Unexpected" slap them in the face and ask them if they expected it.

I took about twenty minutes for the three women to close up the studio. Val and Pixie convinced Tari to let them treat her and her daughter to a late dinner. Tari had missed going out to dinner with Val after class, but after her daughter had been born, she couldn't afford the time or money these social times cost.

It stung her pride a bit to accept the women's offer to pay but it had been impossible to say no. As they were walking out to Val's car the sound of a motorcycle caught all of their attention. Tari felt her chest tighten as memories of her one wild ride played through the back of her mind.

The man who pulled up was right out of a movie trailer for the sexy bad boy. Dark brown hair framed a face which held a short beard that could weaken a woman's knees. He was shirtless with just a black leather vest to decorate muscles which, while a little too bulky for Tari's taste, spoke of hours of hard work.

Pixie squealed and ran to the man, but Tari barely noticed. Her eyes were glued to the ink that covered his chest. A dark, almost scary tattoo version of Pixie faced off over his heart against a roaring, intricately colored dragon. A dragon done in such a familiar style that she couldn't help but be thrown back in time.

Dragon was laid out beneath her like a perfect sexual offering. Tari crawled up his body till she was straddling his hips. She took her time tracing over the swirling bodies of his dragon tattoos with her fingertips, loving the way his muscles twitched under her touch.

Her excitement was slick between them and even though they had just finished, she could feel him hardening against her core again. Tari couldn't resist the urge to move against him; enjoying the sensation of him sliding against her pussy.

She leaned forward, running her tongue around the outline of the dragon's head that wrapped around his left shoulder.

He made a deep sound of contentment running his hands along her hips.

"I think mi reina isn't satisfied yet." The sexy sound of his voice had her nipples hardening.

"Your queen." She nibbled on his neck. "I like that. You said I only had three hours. I'm not going to spend half of that sleeping."

She felt, the tip of his dick brush against her clit and she arched her back in pleasure. Dragon cupped her breasts in his hands, running his thumbs over her tight nipples sending shocks of excitement throughout her body.

"I wouldn't want to shortchange you." She wished she could have a recording of his chuckle to keep her warm at night.

She moved her hips until she felt him lined up, just teasing her entrance. She hovered there enjoying the anticipation and pleasure sweeping through her as he rolled her nipples.

"You are so beautiful, Mami. I wish I didn't have to leave."

Tari didn't want to think about that, she just wanted to feel. Lose herself in the moment with this man who was too quickly becoming part of her heart. She pressed slowly down, trying to memorize the feeling of his cock inside her.

"Don't mind them. Sharp and Pixie are like rabbits in spring every time they get together." Val's voice interrupted Tari's memory.

Pixie had wrapped herself around the shirtless man and the two were kissing like clothes were about to start being discarded. Tari though it was special that the two were so into each other they forgot the world around them. If she was being honest, she also found it really erotic. Watching others always gave her a dirty thrill.

As the two continued, she felt a pang of loss wondering if she and Dragon might have had something that special if fate had been just a little kinder.

"Baby present, y'all need to come up for air," Val teased the two good naturedly.

Sharp swung Pixie around, then finally let her go with a smack on the butt. Tari recognized the crossed rifle and saber design on the back of the vest the handsome man wore and several things clicked into place.

"Dark Zen! I always thought that was an odd name. Do the Dark Sons MC own the studio?" Tari wanted to smack her forehead but luckily holding the stroller kept her from embarrassing herself too much.

Her first college roommate had been obsessed with everything biker. She had often tried to get Tari to let loose and go to some of the wild parties the Dark Sons threw. Tari had never gone but had listened to endless stories and learned more supposed facts about the outlaw lifestyle than any person not living it should need.

Tari had enjoyed the romance novels her roommate had lent her, but the television shows and movies had gotten tiresome after the third viewing. What she did remember was that the Dark Sons was the largest MC in the area and owned many businesses in and around Denver. Her roommate had called them their 'fronts'.

"Yup. I suggested it and my old man Dozer agreed to back it." Val gave her a knowing smile.

The man with the bulging muscles looked over Tari with sharp assessment. She knew she should feel intimidated, yet she felt comfortable. "Now I get to figure out what the hell they were doing. Your man says they gave up too quickly when they found out about the cameras being real. We need to know if it is petty crap or something that needs to be cleaned up." He crouched down smiling at Tari's daughter. "And who is this beautiful girl?"

"I'm Tari and that is my daughter, Citlali."

The big rough man had such a sweet grin on his face when he looked at her child that she immediately felt more friendly towards him. When he straightened and placed his hand on Pixie's baby bump, any woman would be jealous of the obvious love between the two.

"Tari, this is Sharp, Pixie's baby daddy. Vice President of the Dark Sons Denver Chapter and, although strangely shirtless, is usually a good egg."

Tari empathized with the wistful longing she saw on Val's face as she spoke but thought the Southern woman envied the upcoming baby more than the love the two had.

Sharp smiled. "Had an oil change get messy. When Dozer called, I figured Pixie would have a spare shirt so I wouldn't be smelling like my garage all night; while skimming through the footage and searching the place."

Pixie pulled some clothes out of the giant tote she always brought to class and tossed a black shirt to Sharp. She then tossed something black to Val and slipped on a vest of her own. Tari saw that it was a vest similar to Sharp's but instead of the Club name on the back it had Property of Sharp. She remembered the vests were called 'cuts' and, according to her ex-roommate, were sacred to mark a Biker and his Old Lady.

The patches didn't surprise or even offend her as much as she thought they might. The care and love Sharp showed to Pixie was undeniable. So, if they chose to display that in a nontraditional way who was Tari to judge? After Val put on her own vest and Sharp redressed right on the street, Tari studied the trio.

"I feel left out," Tari halfheartedly teased.

"Sharp has plenty of single Brothers." Pixie looked calculating.

"I don't think my package deal would interest them." Tari rocked her now sleeping daughter in the stroller.

"You might be surprised." Sharp leaned over giving Pixie a gentle kiss. "You ladies have fun at dinner."

An hour later the three women were laughing at the antics of Tari's daughter as she sucked on lemon slices and alternately made horrible faces then giggled yelling, "Yum!"

"You are so blessed, Tari. Dozer and I would slay the moon if it meant we could have our own little miracle."

Tari felt awful for the wonderful woman who had slowly become a more than just a student over the last four years. "Do you mind me asking if it is a medical problem?"

"I don't mind. No, the doctors all say we are perfectly healthy but we've tried just about everything, including drugs that made me a raving hormonal lunatic, but nothing worked. We count my cycle every month and have never missed trying on a fertile day. It's heartbreaking every time I realize we've failed again. Eight years is a long time to be disappointed. I think maybe it just wasn't meant to be."

"Eight years?" Tari didn't mean to sound quite so shocked but Val did not look old enough to have been trying so long.

"Dozer met me when I was twenty. We were married the next year."

Tari considered her words carefully. "Twenty-nine isn't nearly old enough to be giving up if you want children. When I was young, I lived all over the world, learned about different cultures, and met so many wonderfully wise people. Can I give you my advice?"

"Of course, sugar."

"Stop worrying. Americans have this competitive drive and anxiety-based culture. That is so harmful to the soul, it is a wonder anyone can do anything being so weighed down by stress. Take six months and just enjoy being in love with your man. Tell him the baby making is off and you just want to enjoy his body's ability to give you orgasms."

Val threw her head back and laughed. "So, I demand orgasms *and* I get a baby?"

"No, you get orgasms. But more to the point, I am guessing it has been a long time since you had sex and didn't think 'I wonder if it will work this time' when he came."

"I wish I could say you were wrong. Six months of just having sex when we feel like it sounds actually kind of nice."

Pixie piped in. "Well, that is how I got knocked up so who knows. How 'bout you, Tari? Was Citlali a result of overindulging in the orgasms your man could give you?"

"Well she wasn't planned and life hasn't been easy, but I wouldn't trade her for anything."

"I don't see a ring and you haven't ever mentioned a man. Does her father help out at all?" Val's question wasn't mean spirited but it was always hard thinking about Dragon.

"It's complicated with a capital C. I don't know where her father is and he doesn't know he has a daughter."

"If you think that is enough information you are crazier than a rocking chair granny. Spill."

So Tari told them about the crazy cheerleaders and talking all night with Citlali's father. Then about the motorcycle ride home that had led to three hours of the most amazing sex of her life.

"Motorcycles are definitely an aphrodisiac," Pixie said with a sigh.

"So he didn't call?" Val asked.

"I don't know. When my parents found out I was pregnant they took everything including my phone, the money they knew about, my clothes, and the years of mementos I had from childhood. Then they shunned me out of the community. If I hadn't had another bank account, and the job at Dark Zen, I don't know what I would have done."

"Why didn't you tell me? I would have helped." Val seemed genuinely upset.

"Before tonight we only ever interacted when most of the class went out together. I counted you as a casual friend, not someone you drop a truckload of issues on."

"I suppose so, but that tale is officially over. We are now sharing and caring friends. So you better call me if you have problems or need someone to watch and pamper your little princess."

Val didn't understand how much her words meant to a woman who had never had a good friend. A few people had been close over the years, but either moving or her own insecurities got in the way. Tari could play confident for short periods of time, but for the most part she was a mess. She tried on some of that confidence and teased her new friend. "I think I would need your number to do that."

Val rolled her eyes and held out her hand. "Phone."

Tari dug out the prepaid phone she kept for work calls. She only had around a hundred minutes left on it but she thought she might have to buy more if she was actually going to have someone to talk with.

Val started typing on the screen and paused. "You only have four contacts on here."

Tari shrugged trying to pretend it didn't matter. Her life was work and her daughter. There hadn't been the time or desire to branch out and make friends.

"Okay, I'm putting mine and Dozer's number in here."

"Put me and Sharp in too. You can call if you ever need a babysitter or just someone to talk with."

Tari gave a small snort watching her daughter make a mess on the table with her fruit slices. "You want me to call the vice president of the Dark Sons MC to babysit my kid?"

Pixie looked at her, offended. "Do you have a problem with the fact that we're part of an MC?"

"No! I meant don't you think he has slightly more important things to do than watch my daughter when my babysitter flakes?"

Both women relaxed, smiling and Tari felt like she had dodged a bullet. "He always knows where I am so if I miss your call he can find me."

Tari doubted she would ever use either man's number but thanked them anyway.

Pixie got a thoughtful look on her face and turned to Val. "Do you think Tek would help her to find her baby daddy?"

"That's an amazing idea." Val clapped in excitement.

"Who's Tek?"

"He's one of the Brothers who among other things helps find people. Mind you it is usually kidnapped kids but he would probably be able to find him if anyone can. Tell us what you know and we'll ask him."

Tari didn't want to get her hopes up but couldn't help the

flutter of hope. "It's embarrassing but I don't know much. He's said he was a Navy SEAL who had family in Denver. He was on leave two years ago. I don't think I even know his real name."

"Do you have a picture?" Val asked.

His face was etched into her mind but she shook her head. "He looked like a blend of Lou Diamond Phillips and Ryan Guzman but more defined."

"That is quite a lust inducing combo." Pixie reached over with a napkin and wiped a streak of fruit pulp from Tari's daughter's face. "What name did he give you and why don't you think it's real."

"Honestly, I didn't think about it till I went to the Navy recruiters to see if they could find him. It seems obvious now that Dragon wouldn't be his real name, but at the time I just thought it was unique."

Both women had stilled, staring at her in disbelief. Tari felt silly enough that she hadn't even considered it might not be his real name. She had spent one wonderful night with the man giving him her body and heart, but she didn't even know who he really was. Pixie almost dove head first into her tote bag and pulled out her phone typing like a mad woman.

"What's wrong?" Tari was confused by the woman's strange reactions.

"Could it be?" Val sounded like she was shocked. She studied Citlali's face as if she was searching it for something.

Pixie made a squealing noise and shoved her phone at the confused mother. Tari took the phone and looked down. The picture was a selfie of Pixie. A gorgeous man sat next to her looking like he was trying to ignore both her and the camera. Tears began blurring her vision as she took in the all too familiar features. It was Dragon.

His midnight hair was just a little longer than she remembered, but there was no denying that face. He was wearing a black leather vest like Sharp, but the name on the front clearly read Dragon. Her hands shook as she looked over to see her new friends grinning like they had just won the lottery.

"I can't believe it. How?" Tari's voice was barely a whisper as she tried to talk around the emotions clogging her throat.

"This is like a fairytale. I have his number let's call him." Pixie was bouncing in her chair.

Shock was quickly replaced by fear. What if Dragon hadn't ever tried to call her? They hadn't made promises that night. She had built up this fantasy in her mind and now faced with the reality all possible problems overwhelmed her.

"No!" Tari practically shouted. She needed a minute to think.

"Why not, honey? Dragon is a good man. He deserves to know he has a daughter."

"You can't just call up a man and say, 'Remember that girl you banged two years ago? Well she's here and surprise, you're a Daddy." All her insecurities scrambled Tari's mind. What if he didn't want to be part of their lives or worse decided he had to, but only out of obligation.

"I guess that would be a bit much." Pixie sounded like a child who had just had their dessert stolen.

Citlali started fussing and Tari picked her up out of the highchair and wiped her face. She used the time to come up with a basic plan; trying to keep what was right for all of them at the front of her mind.

"What if we set up a meeting? Don't tell him it's me."

"Why wouldn't I tell him it's you?"

Tari blew out a frustrated breath. "We don't know if he really was going to call. Most men wouldn't be thrilled by a one-night stand showing up and using his friends to get him to see her again."

Val shook her head. "This is sounding like you don't plan

on tellin' Dragon about his daughter unless he is happy to see you and that just don't fly with me."

Was that what she was doing? He had a right to know. But was no father in Lali's life better than one there only out of obligation? Tari would never force anything on Dragon. She looked down at her daughter before responding.

"Is it selfish of me to want to know if he feels something for me as a woman before letting him know about our daughter?" Her voice was quiet, and she feared their answer.

Val reached out and squeezed her hand. "Oh, precious. We understand but the road to Hell is paved with half-truths and good intentions."

Pixie looked like she was about to cry. "Dragon is a good man. He deserves to know he has a daughter."

"If I swear to tell him within the week can you give me that much time to see how he feels?"

"My gut is tellin' me this is the wrong move, but we can give you one week. Pixie will set up a meet for tomorrow." Pixie nodded and Val reached out and brushed a gentle hand over her daughter's cheek. "But darlin', no matter how much love I have in my heart for you, Dragon is family. In one week, he will know about this precious girl one way or the other."

Chapter 7

Going on blind dates is a good way to reassure yourself that dying alone isn't that bad of an idea.

Dragon had to resist the urge to hang up on the woman who was as close to him as his own sister. "I am not interested in a blind date, *chiquita* and I already have plans for today."

"It's not a blind date." Pixie was adorable when she got frustrated but that wasn't nearly enough for him to give in to her demands.

"You want me to meet a woman at a restaurant. You won't give me her name or any details. I am pretty sure that fits the definition of blind. I am on my way in to spend three hours under Hannibal's needle then I have to ride to Wyoming to start work on Dozer's latest site. I don't have time to meet your friend." Why did women always feel the urge to set up their friends? Dragon hadn't bothered with relationships since he had gotten out of the service.

Women just didn't appeal for more than a momentary distraction. What he wanted was a dream, that instant overwhelming connection that he had only experienced once in his life and he wasn't going to settle for less. So when he didn't feel the connection he quickly bailed. He wasn't as bad as some of the Brothers but he definitely bounced around.

"I'll tell her to meet you at Dark Ink then. I promise you will thank me for it later."

Knowing he was beat since there was no way to stop her, Dragon gave in. "If you want your friend to meet me while I get my Club tattoo worked on fine. But I promise nothing."

"You won't be sorry!" Pixie squealed, hanging up the phone. Dragon loved the crazy chick who had an obsession with running. They had met when he was still a prospect and the two of them often ran together several times a week, even pregnant she could set a decent pace. Dragon had served his first year in the SEALs with her old man, Sharp, and thought it was great the two had found true happiness with each other.

It was just after eleven and Dark Ink was already busy. As the most famous tattoo parlor in the Denver area, they had a waiting list months long if you weren't a member of Dark Sons MC. Dragon had been seventeen when he fell in love with Hannibal's work and waited over a year before he could get his first piece. Since he became a Brother a few months ago both Hannibal and Ink had been working on his back piece and today it should finally be finished. The gorgeous work of art the two had designed had a black Dragon wrapped around a sun with the Club name in gothic script perfectly arching above the sun and under the existing tattooed dragon bodies that ran over his shoulders.

Hannibal walked up and gave him a friendly nod. "Angelique is using my chair so I'm set up in the back." The Brother's Creole accent always reminded Dragon of fun times he had spent with some of his SEAL team on leave in New Orleans.

"Works for me, but Pixie has a friend stopping by to meet me." He tried but failed to hide his exasperation.

"That's what you get for being too nice. Girls try to set you up with their friends. You need to be an asshole like me."

"I may have to try that."

Dragon was face down on the chair two hours later trying to not think about the awkward meeting that was sure to come. What had possessed Pixie to not only try to set him up but be so impatient that she was forcing him to meet the girl today? Telling the mystery woman he wasn't interested without insulting her in the short time he had before he had to hit the road was a feat he wasn't sure he could accomplish.

"Hello boys." Dragon recognized Didi's gravelly voice and prayed she wasn't here to see him. She wasn't exactly a Club sweetbutt but the woman was actively sleeping with multiple Brothers and, while he had shared a woman in the past, it wasn't his thing.

"Hey, *Cher* you're early," Hannibal said with obvious delight. Dragon couldn't help but feel relief that she wasn't here to try to tempt him.

"You know me, I like to come early and often." He heard her heels clicking on the floor over the tattoo machine.

"Now, that is a lovely sight." Dragon wondered what Didi was doing to have Hannibal's voice dropping so low, but didn't bother to turn his head to look. The man was an amazing artist, but Dragon wasn't in the mood to be an audience for the very public sex the man enjoyed sharing with his longtime friend and business partner Ink.

"I can't help myself." Didi's voice had gone breathy. "The thought of you two touching me, filling me, always makes me impatient."

"My hands are busy right now but feel free to get yourself

ready." Hannibal groaned but the feeling of him laying in the last of the color on Dragon's back never paused. The fact the man could keep working when there was obviously something so distracting going on was impressive.

Dragon could hear Didi working herself up and, from the rate of her breathing, the woman would be reaching her climax soon. His body began reacting even though he wasn't looking, or particularly interested, making lying face down uncomfortable.

"*Cristo.*" Dragon was going to need to shift himself soon or risk pain. "How much longer?"

"Five minutes."

"Give me a second to adjust myself."

"I can do that for you, Dragon." The woman should get a job as a phone sex operator she would make a fortune. When Hannibal pulled the needles away, Dragon pushed up and caught site of Didi, naked and teasing her nipples in slow twists. She was beautiful, tattoos covered most of her torso highlighting all the many assets genetics had blessed her with.

Movement behind her caught Dragon's attention and he saw long black hair and red clothes disappearing in a rush back into the main part of the parlor. With the music that was playing he could barely make out the sound of hurrying feet. He dropped back down on the bench and banged his forehead a few times.

"What's up?" Hannibal asked.

"I think the girl Pixie wanted me to meet just came in, got an eyeful, and ran."

"What did y'all do to that poor girl who just left?" Ink's Texas twang preceded him through the curtain. He saw Didi and smiled stepping up and running his hands over her bare shoulders. "Hello, beautiful." He kissed her neck before stepping back.

"Fuck, Pixie's going to be pissed." Dragon was kicking

himself for giving in to the tiny spitfire. He loved his Brothers but anytime more than one of the Dark Sons was present the chance of wild times increased exponentially.

"If that was the woman Pixie was setting you up with, I would be thanking her and hopping on my bike to get to Traker's to try and lure that woman into my bed." Ink was half paying attention as he watched Didi continue to play with herself. The woman literally had no inhibitions and Dragon could respect that even if it didn't appeal. He liked things rough with an edge of kink, but compared to these two he was a priest.

"Traker's?" Hannibal asked as he started back on his work determined to finish up so he could join the play that was starting to get heated.

"Yeah, she was wearing one of their red waitress uniforms and making it look good."

"What did she look like? Maybe we should track her down since the monk here isn't interested."

Dragon was a little tired of the teasing he received for not banging every piece of ass that twitched in his direction. He couldn't even explain to them that after tasting heaven it was hard to find any real enjoyment in fast and cheap. He was amazed Didi didn't seem to care that the men she was about to fuck were talking about going after another woman.

"Tall, lean, Nubian style beauty."

Dragon found himself picturing Tari with her dark amber skin, midnight eyes, and ebony silk hair. He lay back down on the table wanting the tattoo to be done. The slightly uncomfortable arousal he had been experiencing quickly turned to a full blown hard on as he considered maybe meeting this woman wasn't such a bad idea. Easing the ache, he always had when he thought of that night would make the ride to Wyoming much more relaxed.

He ignored the growing sexual banter lost in his own thoughts of the past. His phone rang as Hannibal sat back.

"Done."

Dragon pulled out his phone grimacing when he saw Pixie's name on the screen. He sat up letting Hannibal place ointment and the bandage on as he swiped to answer.

"*Hola querida.*" He winced as the sounds of Didi reaching a climax echoed his words.

"What the fuck, Dragon! You knew Tari was coming and you decided to be fucking some chick when she arrived?"

The name hit him like a knife in the gut. "Tari?"

"Shit. Yeah, Tari. Who I just got a call from saying the meeting didn't work out. From the sound of things, I can understand why she sounded strange."

"That's just Didi." Dragon grabbed his shirt and headed out of the shop with a wave to the two men about to get busy. He strode towards his bike throwing on his shirt and cut as he moved. "Tari, 5'11" black woman with long straight hair?"

"Yes. And I don't care who it was. Why would you be fucking another woman when you knew she was coming?"

His mind was racing. How had Pixie found Nefertari when he hadn't been able to for two years. Hell, he didn't ever even remember telling Pixie about her. If he hadn't told her about Tari how had she known to try and set them up?

"First, I didn't know she was coming. I thought you were just trying to set me up with a random woman. Second, I wasn't fucking Didi, she was putting on a show for Hannibal. Tari must have gotten an eyeful and left."

"So, you didn't talk to her?"

"No, if I had seen her, I wouldn't have let her leave."

"So, you remember her?"

The night they had spent together was burned into his memory. Not just the part in the hotel but the hours talking beforehand. He remembered every smile and laugh he had coaxed out of her right along with the sexy moans she made. "Obviously. Why didn't you tell me she was the one coming?"

"She didn't know if you would remember her and she didn't want me telling you too much."

"Telling me too much about what?"

"I can't, Dragon, I promised, but you need to talk to her. I'll call her. She said she was on her way to work so maybe she's over at the Dark Zen."

"Ink said she was wearing a Traker's uniform." Could she have really been so close this whole time. He never went to Dark Zen or Traker's but he rode by them all the time.

"I don't know how she does it. She must have a second job." Pixie sounded worried and that had all his instincts screaming.

"What aren't you telling me?"

"A lot. Look if you can't find her let me know and I'll call her."

Dragon kickstarted his bike tired of the runaround Pixie was giving him. "Fine."

Traker's wasn't exactly a nice restaurant, in fact Dragon didn't even think it qualified as a dive. The rundown diner was in one of the worst neighborhoods of Denver and mostly served people not particularly concerned with the quality of food as long as it was cheap. The main draw to bring in customers was the barely dressed waitresses in red booty shorts and halter tops.

The thought of his Tari working in a place like that made him ill. What had happened in two years to make a college student working towards becoming a physical therapist need to work two jobs? That one of those jobs was there, meant she had to be desperate for money. Women who worked there were barely one step away from dancing a pole.

Dragon believed a woman had the right to make her living anyway she could but Tari hadn't struck him as someone who would enjoy being looked at like she was entertainment. She was funny and peaceful with a core of strength that anyone could sense if they took a moment to get to know her. She only showed her wild side after drinks and in private. He stepped inside ready to learn that Pixie had been wrong and the woman who worked here wasn't his Tari.

The world seemed to pause as he recognized her standing in front of one of the back tables. She was gorgeous, the dim light of the diner almost glowed off of her midnight hair. The red of her ridiculously sexy uniform stood out like rubies against the velvet dark of her skin. Tari's body was softer than he remembered and it only made her more beautiful. Her body had blossomed and, as he took her in, he imagined exploring those new curves. She turned as if sensing him and their gazes locked like perfect puzzle pieces.

He didn't remember moving but was suddenly in front of her and holding her face in his trembling hands.

"Dragon." Her voice was like whispered music filling a part of him that had felt empty for too long.

"*Mi reina*." He dropped his lips to hers and reveled in the taste of her that was better than he remembered.

Chapter 8

Procrastination is like a credit card: lots of fun till you get the bill

T ari couldn't believe Dragon was really here. Holding her like she was something precious, consuming her like she was the last drink of water in the desert. She had only seen his back earlier, but it was overwhelming being confronted with all of him.

Everything about him was right. She wanted the world to drop away so she could just enjoy him alone. But they weren't alone and he wasn't hers. She used the image of the naked woman earlier to give her the strength to step back. She wasn't a carefree college student anymore and losing herself to a man wasn't a luxury she could indulge in.

"What are you doing here?" Tari's voice was maddingly breathless.

"Pixie told me you were looking for me, of course I came."

His words soothed a hurt part of her heart even if her mind railed against his words. "We knew each other for less than a day two years ago. I don't see where the 'of course' is obvious."

"We were more than that and you know it. I looked for you for months when I got back." He ran a hand down her hair, and she wanted to melt. "I even searched the college directories looking for your name. I can't believe you were here all that time." Dragon leaned forward and kissed her forehead. "Why didn't you tell me you were there at the tattoo shop?"

Were these wonderful words all about their missed connection or had Pixie told him about Citlali? She didn't think the woman would do that but what more could he mean? Tari didn't dare hope to believe he still had feelings for her after all this time. He had been about to fuck another woman less than two hours ago. Remembering the absolute devastation, she felt when she ran from that back room helped straighten her spine. "Was I supposed to offer to join in on the three way or just sit back and watch till you were done."

"I would never share you."

"But sharing that plastic barbie is okay?" Tari knew she sounded like a shrew and took a deep breath. "I have no right to judge you or what you were doing; *lo siento.*"

Dragon ran a hand through his hair with a frustrated sigh. "I know what you think you saw, but I have never been nor will I ever be with Didi. You have no reason to believe me but it's the truth. She is with Hannibal and Ink, not Hannibal and me."

She thought back to what she had seen and heard. Dragon had been face down on the table and she now realized he hadn't been looking at the naked woman. No matter how much Tari wanted to believe him, fear of how much it would hurt if she was wrong, stopped her. The sound of a man yelling at her in rapid fire Spanish broke through her thoughts.

"You want to pick up men like a common prostitute, do it on your

own time! Get that fine ass in gear and pick up food for the paying customers."

Tari rolled her eyes at Jorge, the ancient cook/owner, who was as gruff to customers and employees as his wife Teresa was sweet. The man was a big softy under all the harsh words and bluster so Tari flicked off a mocking salute in his direction before turning back to Dragon.

"Sit at the counter, I'll be right back."

Without waiting for a response, she hurried and brought out the food to her few waiting customers and checked on her others. She returned to find Jorge and Dragon in the middle of a face-off across the counter.

"—you don't speak to my woman like that ever."

"You think you scare me, boy? A real man wouldn't let his woman work in a place where she has to dress like a hoochie."

"Jorge," Tari cut in before things got out of hand. "You're the one who says we have to wear these hoochie clothes." It was an old silly fight. She didn't like looking like a candy cane stripper before the wrapper came off but the tips were nice and Jorge made sure none of the customers got too handsy.

"Yes, but the other *chicas* aren't good girls like you."

"Thanks, Jorge!" Debby shouted from across the room and shot him the finger.

The crusty old owner was right. Most of the women who worked at Traker's were harder and a lot wilder than she was. But Jorge and Teresa had let her work even when her belly had been so big she waddled more than walked. It was a dysfunctional sort of family, but it was all she had.

"Jorge, I'm taking my break. We'll be in the breakroom."

Her boss nodded. He was obviously unhappy, but blessedly silent. She leaned over and gave the grumpy man a kiss on the cheek. Jorge might have a foul mouth and nasty temper but when she had been pregnant, he had shown her his caring side.

Tari knew she couldn't tell Dragon everything here because she would be a wreck if they went down that road. She needed every dollar she made and even the loss of one night's tips could cause her life to spiral out of control. The new sitter was considerably more expensive than the last making things even more precarious. She knew she would have to find someone cheaper soon if she had any hope of affording more than just the bare essentials.

But she could set up a meeting for another time. Let him know that there were important things to discuss. She grabbed Dragon's hand and pulled him behind her to the back, ignoring Debby's waggling eyebrows.

The break room was tiny, smelled like stale fried food and only held a small table and lockers for the waitresses. When the door clicked closed, she turned on Dragon steeling herself not to fold under his powerful gaze. "This is my place of work. You have no right to risk my job by threatening my boss when you don't even know the situation."

His hand wrapped around the back of her neck and he cut off any other argument with a rough demanding kiss. The kiss out front had been soft, like the warm ocean enveloping her, but this was fire and passion. It blanked her mind to all thoughts but him.

His other hand slipped under her shirt and found her nipple, pinching it through the fabric of her bra. He captured her moan of pleasure with his mouth and she felt her core going liquid under his assault.

The feeling of his mouth against hers, his taste, his scent was even better than she remembered. Dragon broke the kiss, pinning her against the lockers with his body, as his hand glided down her stomach sending chills across her skin.

"I have dreamed about the taste of your sweet pussy." His hand slid down into her shorts and slipped into her panties rubbing the cream of her excitement over her clit. "*Mi reina.* You're so wet for me. Tell me what you want."

His fingers slid and circled her clit in teasing strokes. Her whole body was alive with sensations so overwhelming she barely remembered to contain her moans of pleasure. She was panting, wanting to cry out so bad she bit her lip to keep the sound inside.

Dragon's mouth claimed hers again as his finger slid down and thrust inside her. How this man could have her already balancing on the edge of orgasm was magic she wished she could bottle. He chuckled, as she barely held back a cry when he curled his fingers inside her, sending tiny sparks of pleasure shooting through her body.

"Do you want me to make you come? Is your pussy so hungry for me that you will come for me right here?"

"Dragon." His name was a demand and a plea. He was pushing her so high but somehow, she knew he was purposely not pushing her over the edge.

"Beg for me, Tari. Tell me you want me."

"God, yes, Dragon. Please, I want you."

"What do you want?" He thrust his fingers into her and she whimpered trying to get pressure on her clit to take her that last step into an orgasm.

"I want to come. Dragon, I need you." Her whispered voice was filled with her frustration.

Dragon locked their mouths together, his tongue mimicking what his fingers were doing. His thumb pressed down on her clit after a few thrusts and she detonated, her legs going weak. He swallowed her cries as he milked her orgasm, pushing it into another that had her seeing stars.

Tari's breath shuddered as he slowed, staring deep into her eyes. The tingling was bliss as he rubbed gently along her labia, and pulling his hand out of her now soaked panties was almost too much. Her heart and pussy twitched as he brought his fingers to his mouth and sucked the taste of her into his mouth like it was the sweetest of chocolate.

"*Cristo*. You taste even better than I remember, *Mami*."

The endearment sent cold water splashing down her spine. How could she have forgotten she wasn't the only one who would be affected if she took a risk with her heart and failed. There was a very important reason she needed to take things slow. Use her head.

Yet one kiss from him and Tari forgot everything. It had been childish of her to want to see if there was a relationship possible before telling him about Citlali. The chemistry between them meant it would be impossible to find out if there might be more without lying to him for weeks or maybe months.

Tari couldn't risk the damage that might cause to the trust they had to find. Dragon would always be her baby's father. They had to be friends for her sake. Whatever romance might or might not happen between them would either be tainted by lies or forced by obligation.

It would be better not to go there again. She still couldn't tell him tonight but she would force herself to step back. They would be parents and friends. If he even wanted to be either, once he found out.

"I'm glad you came, Dragon." Tari stepped out of his hold straightening her clothes as he chuckled. "But this isn't the time or place to be catching up."

"Embarrassed, *Mami*?" She couldn't help but flinch. "Okay, we'll play this your way. I'll order food and we can talk when you're between customers. Then I'll take you home."

Tari could feel tears forming in her eyes and had to blink them away. Of course, Dragon didn't miss a thing when it came to reading Tari. He was cupping her face with his thumb brushing at her cheek.

"What is it, Tari?"

"I need you to go, Dragon. A lot has happened. A lot I have to tell you, but I can't right now." Tari took in a shuddering breath. "Pixie said you had a job in Wyoming till the weekend. I don't have to work on Sat until three. I'll meet you for breakfast." Dragon looked like he was going to argue. "Please just give me three days. I promise I will explain everything then."

"Don't pull away from me, Tari. I've missed you so much. My job, anything else can wait. I want to know what is putting tears in your eyes."

"I need time. We need to talk and I can't do it here. I need this job. Please, Dragon just give me till Saturday." Tari hated how weak her voice sounded.

Dragon stepped back and ran a frustrated hand through his hair. "All right, *Querida*. I'll wait until then, but this time I'll give you my number. You don't show or call, I will find you."

Tari blinked back tears as he stormed away, praying a few days would be enough for her to figure out what to say.

Chapter 9

You can't turn back time but you can wind that fucker back up.

Dragon spent the three hours riding to Douglas feeling like he was doing the wrong thing. He'd spent so many nights dreaming about finding Tari and, now that he had found her, instead of taking long hours getting reacquainted, he was on his bike traveling to a different state. Why had he agreed to leave her? With the taste of her still on his tongue, only the promise of breakfast in a few days was keeping him sane.

What could be so important and personal that she couldn't talk about it at work and had her pulling away from him in tears? His thoughts were still circling when he pulled up to the hotel where Dozer was staying. Seeing her again had triggered every primal instinct he possessed and he had moved too fast. Tari's body had been in sync every step of the way but obviously her mind hadn't.

Could there be someone else? A wave of fierce possessiveness churned in his gut. She hadn't been wearing a ring on her finger, he wasn't proud of the feeling but he knew anything short of a husband wouldn't stop him. It had been two years so he wouldn't blame her. But she had sought him out, asked to meet with him alone instead of with a group. Which had to mean she was interested in reconnecting, she wasn't the type of woman to do that if she was taken.

Dragon saw Dozer step out of the building. The older Brother's eyes lit up when he saw Dragon sitting on his bike in the lot. Dozer owned and ran DS construction and employed almost half of the Brothers in the Denver chapter. At 49, the Dark Sons' treasurer was an ex-Marine and still in such good shape he could give active-duty members a run for their money. He kept his gray hair regulation length but had a beard that would make Santa proud.

"Wasn't sure you were coming."

Dragon stepped off his bike meeting his Brother with a slap on the back. "It's only seven o'clock. You said we weren't starting demo till tomorrow."

"Val gave me a call. Said they were arranging a reunion for you. She thought you might want to catch up. Told me to have a backup plan."

Dragon envied the close loving relationship the two had but this once wished Val had just kept silent. He respected Dozer but didn't want to have to discuss his personal life with the man. "I did. She didn't."

Dozer raised an eyebrow.

Dragon gave a frustrated growl and gave the shortest and only explanation that made sense to him. "Pixie had her meet me at Dark Ink and she walked in on Didi giving Hannibal a show while I was in the chair. She took off. I caught up with her and pushed too hard. She sent me away saying she needed time. So here I am."

The older man laughed, shaking his head. "Giving a

woman time is like throwing kerosene on a fire. Stupid and fucking dangerous. This girl more than just a fuck?"

It was crazy, but Dragon knew, even though they had so little time together, she was already something vital to him. He had known it two years ago when he had to leave her. Nothing had changed in all those years. Knowing she had been so close made him angry at himself for not asking some of the Dark Sons to help in his search for her.

He took a deep breath determined not to make that mistake again. "Yeah. She's more than that."

"Good, because I already have a replacement for you here. You can head back to Denver, clean up your shit, and help me out with something else."

"Didn't know you had any jobs going in Denver."

"It's Club business not construction work."

As an officer for the Dark Sons MC, Dozer could pull resources as he saw fit. Every Brother had to help out when needed and, in return, they got a monthly income. Extra jobs, outside of the usual, meant extra income but Dragon wasn't sure if this request was helping out or a job, not that he would say no either way.

"What do you need?"

"I need you to clean up the absolute clusterfuck at Dark Zen."

From what Dragon knew the business wasn't anything more than a cash neutral spa the Club bought, to have something to make the old ladies happy. Pixie had said Tari was working there but he didn't even know what she did. "What kind of clusterfuck can a spa get into?"

Dozer rolled his eyes. "It was my mistake not paying attention to that shit. But seriously, who the fuck could have known a yoga studio and holistic living spa could be a front for a major heroin distributor."

"Seriously?"

Dragon was surprised that any dealer would have the balls to use one of the Dark Sons' businesses for anything. Tari worked for a place that was dealing heroin. Was that the major talk they had to have? If his woman had gotten dragged down into something like selling drugs, all her fear and nervousness made sense. It wouldn't matter to him what kind of trouble she was involved in. If he couldn't fix it, one of his Brothers would know what to do.

"Sharp found enough heroin hidden in the shop to supply most of Denver's addicts for a week. He cleared it out and pulled all the books and shit in the safe, too, which is good because after he left, masked assholes broke in and trashed the place."

"*Cristo.*"

"Christ is right. Sharp has done a quick look but he has his own garage to worry about. Since you have that fancy business degree, I figured using you for manual labor was a waste of talent."

It surprised him that Dozer knew he had earned a Masters in accounting while on active duty since he had never mentioned it to anyone. The exact precision of math and finance had always been a way to get his mind off of the messy reality that was life. It had taken him nine out of the ten years he was on active duty but he had left the service with a piece of paper that meant he could get a job outside of manual labor if he wanted. Which he hadn't.

"Who told you?"

"I'm the treasurer of our chapter. We own over fifty businesses in the Colorado area. I may mostly focus on D.S. Construction but who do you think has to make sure all the companies not actually run by Brothers keep making money?"

"And that means you know about my degree how?"

"I know every resource available to the Club. Before we even asked you to prospect, we knew more about you than your own mother." Dozer seemed amused by his ignorance, but Dragon was stunned. It made sense that the MC ran background checks, he had never considered what that could mean.

He knew the Club was big and took in enough money that the monthly stipend for being an active Brother was enough that it could support a modest living. Most of them did extra work to supplement but it never occurred to him that the primary source of that regular money was legitimate businesses.

"So, you want me to take over running the shop?"

"If you're interested. But right now, we need someone to figure out just how bad the books were cooked and if we have any other surprises coming our way. The pay will be better than you would have gotten here swinging a hammer for me."

Dragon wasn't really worried about that. He didn't need much. His thoughts froze for a minute. If Tari was going to be a part of his life, he needed to start thinking more long term. He had only been living moment to moment since he left the service. The future now might actually contain something to look forward to.

"I'm in."

"Good. Get back to Denver and make sure that woman doesn't think you right out of her life."

Chapter 10

What doesn't kill you…

Tari got off the bus exhausted. Thank God, Citlali didn't wake when she transferred her to the stroller. It was just after ten and if her daughter woke up now it would be hours before she settled down again. After the emotional rollercoaster of this afternoon, and a tiring shift on her feet, all Tari wanted to do was settle down into a bath and go to sleep.

Footsteps echoed her own as she started off towards home. A quick glance over her shoulder had fear spiking in her throat. Two local gangbangers were shadowing her steps about ten feet back. After paying the babysitter she only had a few dollars of her tips left. If they tried to shake her down, she knew it wouldn't be enough. They were smaller men with tattoos and colors that marked them as members of the Jacks. Tari had heard enough rumors of the cruelty it required to become a member and quietly prayed this wouldn't become a confrontation.

Tari hunched her shoulders regretting not changing fully before leaving work. She almost never left in the tiny shorts they had to wear, changing instead into old comfy jeans. However, tonight, she was still wearing the red halter top that showed too much cleavage to make her comfortable in this situation. Why men insisted on catcalling and harassing a woman, especially one with a baby was baffling, but from the leering looks on the two men's faces she was sure she would have to put up with it again tonight.

Tari hoped the three blocks to her apartment was long enough that they could get their laughs and leave her be. If they followed the whole way she would go into the manager's office that doubled as a convenience store until they hopefully got bored and left.

The rough grip that wrapped around her neck shocked her so much that she was halfway down the alley before she started fighting back. She was thrown against a wall and pain exploded as one of the men punched her; causing her to stumble and fall to her knees.

Her cry for help was cut off when the same man kicked her in the face and her head hit the wall; the world shattered for a moment into prisms of light. Her breath rushed out of her as he kicked her several times in the chest and head. Her cracked ribs hurt more as she hit the ground and she tried to crawl through the pain to protect her daughter.

"Little snitch. No one fucks with Jacks' business."

He pinned her legs down by sitting on them. His dirty hands easily ripping the fabric of her top exposing her breasts. Tari's mind swirled, lost in pain and confusion.

"Please, I didn't do anything!" The world blurred and tilted, her words sounding like they came from far away.

She felt more than saw the knife running down her neck

leaving pain and a bloody trail as it ran over her breast and onto her stomach. She couldn't help the scream that bounced off the walls when he pushed the blade in and she felt it tearing through muscle. He laughed and ran the blade down the other side of her body repeating the action. This time she heard her scream echoed by her daughter. Terror gave her strength and she thrashed, trying to get to her baby and somehow protect her from what was happening.

"Fifi told us everything. Your stupidity cost us over a hundred grand in product."

He ran the blade across her stomach slowly. Again, and again she screamed for help that wasn't coming. Her attacker's face showed no pity, only sick enjoyment as he took his time cutting bloody trails into her.

"Please, please don't hurt my baby." The pain was so great that her mind barely registered the amount of blood that was now pooling on and around her, but the gray and black fog around her vision told her that her time was running out.

"You and your little brat are going to be left as examples for what happens to people who cross the Jacks."

Tari ignored the pain, thrashing as if she wasn't a mass of bleeding wounds. She had to find a way to save her baby. Had to find some power that would make these evil men not kill her daughter. A desperate idea formed in her mind and she prayed as she spoke it would be enough.

"You hurt my baby and the Dark Sons will destroy you!"

"What did she say?" The man not treating her like a pincushion asked.

The hesitation in his voice gave her hope. Tari tasted the copper of her own blood in her mouth. She could just see her daughter in the stroller pushed up against the side of the alley screaming her terror into the night. She had to make these men believe her.

"She's lying."

She shook her head. "Her father is high up in the Dark Sons. You do one thing to her and he won't stop until he finds you." Tari had no idea how high up Dragon was but she did know one man who was right at the top. She didn't think he would mind her using his name if it meant saving Citlali. "Sharp is her father. He's the vice president." She threw in the last in case it wasn't common knowledge among criminals who was who.

Her attacker stood cursing and she rolled to her side trying to push through the pain that wanted to drag her into unconsciousness and find something she could do.

"Sharp is a fucking psycho, Chobo. I ain't touching shit that belongs to him."

Tari almost found it funny that a man who had just watched his friend Chobo slash a woman repeatedly would call anyone else a psycho.

"She's lying. Fifi said this bitch wasn't associated with those fuckers."

The sound of Citlali's crying gave Tari the strength to dig down into her pocket and pull out her phone. The two started arguing and didn't notice her motion. Fumbling for a few seconds she somehow dialed the number Pixie had programed into her phone. The sound of Sharp answering had her crying out in relief. His deep gravel voice the sweetest sound to her ears.

"Sharp."

"Help—" she screamed before Chobo finally noticed what she had done and snatched the phone out of her hand.

"Who's this?" Chobo snarled into the phone before he quickly hung up. "Fuck!" He threw the phone.

Tari's phone hit her in the face and she clutched it, unable to do any more than struggle for air as her vision continued getting blurry at the edges.

Chobo paced a few steps away and punched a wall. Tari

lost her grip on consciousness for a moment and only snapped back when she felt someone pawing at her neck. "No pulse, fuck. Well the bitch is dead she won't be able to tell anyone shit. Leave the kid. We need to get out of here before they trace her down."

She forced herself to remain still until she heard the two men running away. She would have sobbed in relief if she could have spared the breath. Her baby was crying. Citlali wasn't safe yet. Home was one block away if she could get her daughter there someone would come.

Tari managed to get to her knees, then used the wall of the alley to stumble to the stroller. Light faded in and out as she forced her body to move. Everything focused down to moving just a bit closer to safety. She wouldn't fail her daughter. Ringing, car honking, crying, all of the noises meant nothing. She focused on just getting each step closer to home.

The few people on the street she saw looked away knowing who had hurt her and not wanting to get involved. How could fear make people so callous? Her top was ruined flashing everyone but she didn't care. Nothing but pushing the stroller one more step mattered. Blood dripped down the smooth plastic and onto the fabric of her daughter's seat. Time seemed to stretch and flow as the sounds of her daughter's cries lessened and the ringing kept stopping and restarting its incessant noise.

Stumbling and trembling with fatigue she somehow managed to make it to her first-floor apartment and get her daughter inside. Safe. She had reached safety. Her fingers shook as she locked the door and legs that couldn't hold her anymore collapsed. Citlali was quiet and the ringing started again. Only then in the quiet of her apartment did Tari realize it was coming from the phone still somehow clutched in her hand.

She hit the accept key and was happy to hear the enraged voice like flames over water come through the speaker.

"Who the fuck is this?"

"It's Tari." Her voice echoed oddly. Her vision now reduced down to tiny pinpricks of light.

"Tari? What's going on? Talk to me." His voice was gentle now and Tari was glad that Pixie had someone who was both scary and sweet.

It was so hard to focus. She knew she had to tell this sweet man something. Something about the man she was never going to hold again. "Tell Dragon. Tell him I'm sorry." Sorry she had pushed him away for fear. Sorry she would never get to see the wonder in his eyes as he saw the miracle that was his daughter.

"Sorry for what, honey? Where are you?"

Yes, she had to tell him to come. Where to go to save her daughter.

"Home. Lali is safe but I'm… He's going to have to…" Her mind was misfiring and she tried to hold it together. There was one last thing she had to do. One last thing she had to say before the angels took her. "Promise me you'll tell him. She's his daughter… someone has to… He– he has to keep her safe."

Tari's phone rolled from her hand to the ground.

Chapter 11

A real man is like an oyster – Hard on the outside but soft where it counts.

I t was almost midnight when Dragon felt his phone vibrate. He was twenty minutes outside Denver and when he pulled his phone out, he saw he had missed four earlier calls, all from Sharp. He always put his phone on vibrate but sometimes on long rides he missed calls. A few guys had Bluetooth units, but he had never thought the bulk of a helmet was worth the expense.

Pulling over to the side of the road Dragon answered as he stopped.

"What's up, Sharp?"

"Where are you?"

"Just north of Denver. Why? What's wrong?"

"You need to come over to Denver Health."

Dragon gripped his phone a little too tightly. "Is Pixie and the *bebe* okay? What happened?"

"She's fine." Sharp took a deep breath and Dragon felt his stomach roil. "Your woman's been hurt."

"Tari? *¿Qué mierda pasó?*" Dragon yelled his fear and temper overwhelming his control.

"It's too much for the phone and she may not have much time; just get here."

Dragon shoved his phone in his pocket and rode like the fires of Hell were chasing him. What the fuck could have happened to her in the few hours he had been gone. If his leaving had been the cause of her getting hurt, he would never forgive himself. Images of car wrecks and robberies flashed through his mind so quickly he was worried he wouldn't be sane by the time he reached her.

He raced into the parking lot of Denver Health twenty-five minutes later and saw Flak, the newest Dark Sons' prospect, waiting by the entrance. He barely stopped his bike before jumping off knowing the man would take care of it and raced inside.

Grinder, one of the Brothers he was closest to, waved him over to the elevator. The doors closed on them and Dragon was afraid to speak.

"She's in surgery. Everyone is up in the waiting room. We've told them you are her fiancé and Cheryl brought over a Healthcare proxy listing you as agent so they won't give you a hard time. Tek also did some magic and upgraded her health care coverage so they won't hesitate when choosing what to do."

How his Brothers had pulled everything together so quickly for a woman he hadn't even told them about was over-whelming. He would find a way to pay them all back somehow but right now he needed to know about Tari.

"What happened?"

"She was attacked near her home. We have Brothers combing the streets to find out what happened but so far no one is talking. From what Puck said she's in bad shape, they've had her in surgery for about two hours."

The doors opened and Dragon could tell by the gathering of his Brothers where he had to go. He walked fast knowing there was nothing he could do but needing to be there.

"How did you even know she was hurt?"

"She called me." Sharp stepped out of the doorway that must lead to the waiting room. Six of his closest Brothers were inside along with a few old ladies.

"Why did she have your number?" And why hadn't she called him? Everything was still a jumble of confusion and he needed to sort it out.

"Pixie gave it to her the other night. Thank fuck she did. I don't ever want to get a call like that again but she'd probably be dead right now if she hadn't."

Another thing he had to be grateful to Pixie for. Though from the grim looks on everyone's faces Tari might not survive even with that stroke of luck.

Dragon listened, his whole body vibrating with tension as Sharp told the story of getting the call and knowing Tari was in serious danger. Tek had gotten her home address from Dark Zen's records and called Puck, a prospect that lived nearby. Puck had gone over and found her unresponsive in a pool of her own blood looking like she had been beaten badly. When he couldn't wake her, he had called an ambulance. Sharp had organized everything from there.

"So, I have to talk to the nurses. Find out what is going on. What do the cops know?" Dragon felt like he'd been hit by a truck. He had just found Tari again and he might lose her despite everything his Brothers had done.

"Deep is handling the cops for now. Val just got an update. Surgery is going well but it will be a few hours before they can tell us for sure. There is something else you need to know."

Sharp looked uncomfortable and it wasn't an expression Dragon had ever seen on the man's face.

His friend stepped aside and Dragon could see more clearly into the waiting room. Pixie and Cheryl were sitting next to Val who was bouncing a wiggling, cranky, baby girl on her lap. There was no question in Dragon's mind this beautiful child belonged to Tari. She had chin length, straight black hair held back by a yellow flowered clip. Her skin was lighter than her mother's but no one could deny the sparkling dark eyes were an exact copy of Tari's.

Dragon stood there motionless as Val looked up and gave him a welcoming smile. She stood, transferring the girl to her hip with no effort. He had trouble catching his breath as the pair moved closer.

"Dragon," Val said in a gentle voice. "This is your daughter, Citlali."

The little girl clapped her hands and held them out to him. "Up!"

Dragon felt his knees buckle a bit and Grinder and Sharp grabbed his arms keeping him upright. Their small chuckles snapped his mind back into gear and he stepped forward to catch the perfect little angel in his arms.

Citlali fit like she was meant to be there. Her little head fell onto his shoulder and snuggled in close to his neck. Children always made him feel awkward since he was so big, but Citlali was different. She was his. And he was hers.

"You're a natural." Val smiled, and much to Dragon's chagrin, pulled out her phone and snapped a picture.

His daughter. Of all the things he had imagined Tari had to tell him, not once had the thought of a child entered his mind. Guilt swamped him. He had left her without any way to contact him. He had selfishly left thinking she would wait for his call never thinking once that she would need him. How different would things be if he had taken five seconds to write down his number.

He didn't question that this was his daughter. He could feel the connection and knew in his soul that this little princess was his. He tried and failed to keep his emotion out of his voice as he faced Val.

"How long have you known?" Dragon wanted to be mad but something about the sleepy little girl who was settling in quietly on his shoulder made that impossible.

Pixie stood up looking guilty. "We only found out yesterday but she wanted to be the one who told you."

"She didn't. I would have never left for Wyoming if I'd known."

"We know, sugar. If I had known her and that sweet child were living in East Colfax I would have made her call you and tell you that night." It looked like everyone, including Val was feeling responsible.

East Colfax wasn't exactly a war zone but the thought of Tari having to live there with his daughter was unacceptable. They all moved into the waiting room and Dragon found himself slowly rocking the little girl who was quickly becoming dead weight.

"Say the word and we'll get her moved into one of the apartments on the compound," Sharp offered.

The compound was a couple hundred fenced acres east of Denver that held the main Clubhouse. The Dark Sons officers all had houses built on the property along with a few other members. They had also built a two-story apartment complex with one- and two-bedroom apartments that were used by prospects and active-duty Brothers who didn't have their own places. Dragon had been living in one of the single bedroom units from the time he had started prospecting when he was still active-duty.

His first instinct was to move them both into a two-bedroom unit, but didn't know if the independent woman now fighting for her life would appreciate it.

Grinder spoke up, "Puck is watching her place but he had to bust in a window to get to her. If we don't move her shit, she won't have anything to come back to."

"It's a good idea." Dragon rubbed his daughter's back. His daughter. The thought was so foreign, but right.

"Okay, I'll get the Brothers on that." Grinder pulled out his cell and walked out of the room.

He looked at the woman who had become like his own sister over the last few months. "Did she tell you why she disappeared? I tried to find her but she vanished."

Pixie nodded. "It's going to be a long night. Let's sit down and I'll tell you what I know."

<hr />

An hour later, Dagon sat with his daughter sleeping on his chest. He was absolutely floored by everything he had learned. A nurse had come in, and after Cheryl gave her the fake legal papers, told him everything. Tari's wounds were less severe than originally believed. Most of the bleeding had been caused by superficial wounds. The surgery had been to relieve pressure from cranial bleeding but the nurse said it went well. The damage to her head was the most severe, from the beating she had received, and they weren't sure if there would be brain damage once she woke up. The doctor would come see him once all the lacerations were attended to and hopefully be able to give him more news.

The woman he intended to claim as his had been fighting for her life while he was nowhere to be found. Just like before he had left her alone. When she woke up it didn't matter what they had to face, and he would make sure she understood she would never be alone again. He now was responsible for a precious little girl and finding, and destroying, whoever had done this to her mother. Pulling out his phone he dialed the one person he needed more than anyone else in this moment.

"*¿Bueno?*" A tired woman's voice answered on the third ring.

"*Te necesito, Mamá.*"

Chapter 12

Parenthood is the scariest hood you will ever go through.

His mother had come an hour ago, giving her love and strength to him without reserve. She had calmly, and with genuine warmth, accepted the fact he was a father and the sleeping angel was her newest granddaughter. Val and his mother had taken the sleeping Citlali back to his place to sleep leaving him to await news of Tari's condition.

The only people left in the waiting room were Sharp and Hannibal who had shown up an hour ago to relieve Grinder. It was after three in the morning when a tired surgeon finally came through the doors.

"Gabor Rios?" The surgeon looked between him and Hannibal, rightly assuming the name likely belonged to the man with skin darker than milk.

Dragon stood up, fearing the look on the man's face. Had

something gone wrong? He had to believe Tari was alive. Something inside him would know if she was dead, wouldn't it?

"Ms. Johnson's surgery went well but there was extensive blood loss from the many lacerations to her chest before she got here. The internal bleeding and damage to the brain from the blunt force trauma was significant and we had to drill Burr holes to relieve the pressure. Unfortunately, she didn't wake up after the procedure and has slipped into a coma. We do see mild responses to physical stimuli so we are hopeful she will wake given time. Until then there is no way to tell the level of brain damage that occurred. As for the rest of the injuries, most of her lacerations were superficial and did not require stitches so we expect her to have minimal scarring."

"Can I see her?"

"Of course. I'll send a nurse to let you know when they have her in a room."

"Thank you."

Dragon didn't know if he should feel happy or scared. Brain damage could mean anything. She was alive, but would she be the same person he knew before? Hell, he hadn't known her long enough to be sure if he would even notice if she changed. Doubt and fear circled in his brain.

"*Gabor*, and I thought my name was bad." Hannibal surprised a laugh out of him which was probably the point.

"It is Mayan. My mother says it means bravest warrior."

"Guess it's slightly better than Henri, which I'm pretty sure is Creole for 'boy who gets his ass kicked till puberty'."

When the nurse came back and said only two people could visit, Sharp said goodbye and promised to check in later. Dragon had heard what had happened to Tari, but nothing prepared him for the impact of seeing her lying on the hospital bed.

He saw bandages and tubes crisscrossing her chest and stomach before the nurse pulled up the sheet. Her face was swollen, hiding all the beauty he knew lay beneath. A small tube ran along her cheek disappearing into her nose. Her dark skin hid some of the bruising but swollen patches of black covered her face and arms. Her lovely black hair was pulled up in a messy bun revealing a shaved patch and a small bandage.

"She looks strong." Hannibal put a comforting hand on his shoulder.

"She is. The first time I met her she was facing down a squad of blonde bitches who wanted her to be their token black girl."

Hannibal gave a small smile. "My mama would love her. She has no time for fools or those who put up with them."

"*Mi madre también.*" Dragon wanted to kill whoever had done this. He wanted it to be slow and painful. "Am I a fool? I've spent less than twenty-four hours with Tari and it feels like a part of my soul is lying there."

"*Non.* You're not a fool. When the right woman comes along in five minutes or five years, it makes no difference, you grab on and enjoy that ride."

"That's what you do with Didi?" Dragon teased, doing his best to pull out of the melancholy that was threatening to overwhelm him.

"Nah. Though she is one hell of a ride. If Ink and I ever find that one, you can be damn sure she ain't going to get away."

"Mama, up!" Dragon sighed and pulled his daughter back from the edge of the bed.

"Mama can't get up right now."

"Papa, up!" Lali stretched up high reaching and wiggling her adorable little fingers. Her hair was flying out of the clips he had put in earlier and the outfit she was wearing was the fourth of the day. If the little angel spilled one more thing, he was thinking naked might be the best option.

He smiled and bent down to pick her up, and just like the last fifty times they played this game, she dodged him and bent at the waist, giggling. "Down Dog."

"And you are an adorable little dog." He gripped her by the hips, and swung her a few times before putting her back on her feet.

"It looks like you got this Daddy thing down, Dragon." Val's voice was a welcomed sound.

"Glad I'm fooling someone." Dragon ran his hand through his hair. How had Tari done this alone for almost two years? He had Val and his mom helping him out, and he was barely keeping up with things. The books he was supposed to be reviewing only got looked at at night when either woman came and picked up his little girl. Doing her hair was like wrestling an oiled pig and he somehow always managed to have her crying before all the knots were out.

"Don't you fuss. You're doing a fine job. It's only been three days, you'll get the hang of it."

Three days without any progress with Tari. Three days and no closer to knowing who had attacked her. It took everything he had not to let his little girl see how angry he was.

"Well today Lali is teaching me all about up and down, dog and cat, and telling me very seriously something that sounds like not my tea."

Citlali put her hands together and bowed adorably. "*Namate*, Papa."

His heart melted every time she called him Papa. He swept his daughter up in his arms and gave her a kiss as Val burst out into laughter.

"She is as cute as a kitten in yarn." Val put her hands together, eyes sparkling with laughter. "*Namaste*, Lali girl."

"Nantie Val!" Lali dove for Val and Dragon had to scramble not to drop her.

Val scooped the girl out of his arms and kissed her cheeks. "Have you been teaching your papa Yoga?"

"Yesss!" The tiny bundle of energy bobbed her head enthusiastically.

Things clicked together and Dragon chuckled. "That makes so much more sense."

Dragon slipped Citlali's headband back onto her head and picked her up. "Give your mama a kiss goodnight, *Princesa*."

He leaned his little girl over so she could kiss her mother's forehead. Today had been a good day for him and Lali. Only two outfit changes and not a single tear during hair brushing time. Six days of being a father and he had learned things he never knew he needed to know. The only thing that could have made the day better was if Tari had woken up.

"Come to *Abuela*, sweetheart."

Dragon handed off his daughter to his mother, then kissed them both on their cheeks. "I'm going to stay a bit."

"Don't you worry, *mijo*. We'll be fine."

"I know, Mama."

The sound of his daughter's voice faded as they walked away and Dragon settled himself next to the bed. The swelling had gone down and Tari looked almost as if she was just sleeping. He took her hand into his own squeezing it softly.

"I don't know how you did this by yourself for years. I can barely keep up with her and I have Mama and Val giving me breaks and my Brothers making sure I have nothing to worry about. You are so damn strong, *mi reina*, you can beat this. You will never be alone again if you give me a chance."

Citlali and Tari were now dug deep into his heart and he could not imagine a world where he didn't get to raise the joy, that was their daughter, with her. Alone in the room, Dragon let his head drop and the tears flow freely into the starched white sheets.

Chapter 13

If this is a dream, I will kill the person who wakes me up.

Everything felt wrong. Her skin itched and she was sweating even though the room wasn't hot. Strange sounds were all around her, making Tari realize this couldn't be her bedroom. Why wouldn't her eyes open? Her heart raced, and she slowly became aware her whole body ached like she was getting over the worst of flus.

Voices became clearer, adding to her confusion. She knew that sweet southern twang, it belonged to one of her yoga students Val. The woman was a delight and Tari had always thought she would make a good friend, but between two jobs and taking care of her daughter, there had never been time.

It made no sense the woman would be wherever she was sick. A second voice spoke, and even without seeing his face, Tari knew she was dreaming. The deep, rich tones that held a slight Spanish accent had haunted her nights for almost two years. The memories of his laugh and touch, both gentle and rough, had helped her stay sane when the world became harsh.

She saw echoes of his face in her daughter's, and took comfort in that when the little girl refused to sleep. For what seemed like the millionth time, Tari thought about what life could have been like if only she had asked more questions on that wonderful night. What kind of woman sleeps with a man and doesn't know his last name? Who doesn't say, 'Dragon is a cool nickname but what's your real name' before letting him inside your body?

Tari needed to see his face again; wanted to know his touch. She fought to open her eyes, fearing it would end this beautiful dream, but hoping before she woke back in her tiny apartment, she would get a glimpse of him one more time.

It felt like sand was holding her lids closed but she blinked it away and fought against the too bright light. Plain white walls held a painting of flowers she didn't recognize.

"Sweet Virgin Mary, I think she's waking up," Val said.

Tari's vision was suddenly filled with exactly who she had prayed for. His features were even more beautiful than she had remembered. Regal sharp lines, deep almost liquid brown eyes, and lips that were so soft and full they begged for kisses and other naughtier things. Tears began to blur her vision and she knew this dream wouldn't last much longer.

"Just one more kiss." Tari's voice was harsh and filled with pain, but her dream man understood because his lips were claiming hers a moment later.

His lips were so gentle and even more sensual than she remembered. Her body wouldn't move, but she reached toward him with her heart and opened her mouth to deepen the kiss. His tongue swept in and Tari found it strange that her imagination made him taste like ham and mustard since she absolutely despised the condiment.

He ended the kiss slowly moving back so she could see his

face through her tear blurred eyes. She licked her lips almost laughing. "I hate mustard."

His laugh, choked with emotion, filled the room. "I'll remember that."

"Will you tell me your real name before I wake up?"

Tari's voice was slowly regaining strength, but her body in this dream was still sluggish and wouldn't follow her desires. She wanted to pull him down and relive all the wonderful things he could do to her body. Rediscover the passion that had made her lose her sense all those years ago.

"Gabor. Gabor Rios, *mi reina*. But you are awake, this isn't a dream."

"*Que?*" This had to be a dream. Nothing made sense. Val, and her big red hair, stepped into view on the other side of her. She was wearing a green top with rhinestones peppered along the scooped neck.

"He's right, sugar. You're in the hospital." Val patted her arm but it felt distant like there were several plush blankets between them.

"I don't understand. Why are you here? Where is here?" Her brain raced and then terror had her stomach pitching. "Lali! Oh my God, *where is* Citlali?"

She tried to sit up but her muscles barely twitched.

"Citlali. You want to know where our daughter is?" Dragon looked confused and Tari was too scared to understand his confusion. She nodded, praying her daughter was okay.

"She's with her *abuela*. She's safe. I'll have Mama bring her over. She's been visiting you every day."

"You know about her? *How did you find us?*" Things weren't adding up right. Even now that she was thinking, parts of her memory were still dark and fuzzy. She tried again to sit up but her body still refused to obey. "*What's wrong with me?*"

Dragon looked between her and Val, his eyes wide. "She is talking but not making sense. What do we do?"

"I'll go get the doctor." Val hurried away.

Tari's mind was a jumble of conflicting needs. Dragon was here like some miracle out of a storybook. She wanted to know how this was possible. Her body was acting like she was drugged: slow and muffled. She was in a hospital and she didn't know why or how she had gotten here.

Dragon stroked her cheek and she couldn't stop the tears that were slowly soaking her face.

"Everything's going to be okay. You're alive, our daughter is perfect, and everything else we can figure out."

He knew about Citlali? How? His words were comforting but caused more confusion than relief. Why was he here by her side acting as if they were more than strangers with amazing chemistry? What wasn't she remembering?

A doctor came in the room, his face had a big smile. He was somewhere in his late forties with slightly graying brown hair and gentle eyes.

"Ms. Johnson it is good to see you awake. I'm Dr. Marks, I'm the neurologist on your case."

"It's nice to meet you."

"What's wrong with her?" Dragon's voice was filled with strain. Tari looked between him and the doctor with growing worry.

"Let me do a quick exam and then you can ask any questions you might have."

She had plenty of questions but had no idea where to start. A nurse came in and made Dragon leave. Seeing him walk out the door caused Tari anxiety, but she held onto the belief he wouldn't just disappear.

They proceeded to run through a series of tests that involved poking and prodding every part of her body. Her body and its weak responses terrified her but seemed to please the doctor. Bandaged cuts covered her stomach and chest, two particularly nasty ones ran all the way up to her neck. Moving anything took a struggle so hard that sweat was beading on her forehead and body like she had run a marathon.

"The sluggishness you are feeling in your muscles is normal because of the drugs we've had you on to prevent spasms and seizures while you were in the coma. We'll stop those and check you out in a few hours but you seem to have good nerve responses so you should have full mobility."

"What happened *to me*?"

"Just a few more questions, then I will explain what I can."

He ran her through a lot of questions that ranged from what she thought was today's date, to shape recognition, and simple math problems. Tari had been taking some pre-med classes before her life had taken its drastic detour and she recognized he was trying to establish her mental acuity.

"Do you want your fiancé in here for the discussions in case he has any questions?"

"My fiancé?" Was he talking about Dragon?

"You are a very lucky woman. Your friends and he have been here every moment we would let them in." The doctor had a faint New England accent making her think he was from Connecticut or somewhere near there.

The nurse smiled. "We will miss Mrs. Rios and Pixie's baking when you go home. I swear I've gained five pounds in five days."

Mrs. Rios, Pixie? The only Pixie she knew was a new student Val had brought with her a few weeks ago. She didn't have friends who would visit unless it was some of the waitresses from Traker's and that didn't seem likely.

"Uhm, yes, Dragon can come in."

"What about, Sueann?" the nurse asked.

"Who?" She was positive she didn't know anyone with that name.

"The red-headed woman who was in here earlier. She used to be a nurse here so I know she'll ask." Janis looked concerned.

"Val?" Tari knew the fun-loving woman was a nurse, and having someone with more medical knowledge couldn't hurt, but why had the woman called her Sueann? "Sure."

Janis laughed. "I forgot the people in her husband's Club call her Valkyrie. It fits. She was definitely hell on wheels while still being nice. We will miss her."

When the nurse opened the door, Dragon immediately came to her side and took her hand. His eyes studied her like he was afraid she was going to vanish which was amusing since she felt the same way. The doctor sat on a rolling chair and took a deep breath.

"To answer your question from earlier Ms. Johnson, you were brought in with a significant number of lacerations to the abdomen as well as trauma to your ribs, arms, and head. The damage to your head caused a hematoma and they had to drill a hole to reduce pressure on your brain."

"I don't remember any of that." She had seen the healing wounds but even they hadn't painted the picture the doctor's words had just etched into her mind.

"You were in a coma for six days. We will need to do more in depth testing, but you seem to have minor paraphasia and amnesia that covers about two months before you were admitted."

"What is paraphasia?" Dragon asked while Tari was still trying to process what was going on.

"It is a condition where a person unknowingly says a nonsense word when speaking rather than the word intended." The doctor looked down at his clipboard. "For example, when I showed her a circle she called it a *dayeera*."

"*Dayira* means circle in Arabic." Tari defended herself.

"Interesting. Did you mean to speak Arabic?"

"Well, no, but the word is not nonsense." Tari didn't like the fact her brain and her body weren't working. She had always kept herself in good shape, eating right, and considered herself intelligent. The fact that both things might be taken from her was terrifying.

"When I asked you how many siblings you had, you said, *geen*."

"That is none in Dutch."

"How many languages do you speak?"

"Ten, if you include English. *Does this mean I don't have* para-phasia?" Tari didn't want to have something wrong with her brain. Plenty of bilingual or multilingual people switched between languages without thinking about it. She usually only did that with Spanish since she had primarily grown up speaking that and English. But she had been fascinated with learning languages when she grew up so it wasn't impossible for it to happen with another language.

Dragon squeezed her hand and she saw his face was worried.

"The only words you just spoke that were in English were English and paraphasia. Try it again but relax and try to focus on English."

She did, forming each word as she spoke it.

"Ten languages is very impressive. I'm going to get you the name of someone who specializes in Aphasia and related speech disorders. This, along with the amnesia, may be a temporary thing or they may be something that is now part of your life."

"Will she ever remember what happened? Who did this to her?" Dragon asked.

"With retrograde amnesia it is difficult to say anything definitively. She may wake up tomorrow with total recall or she might never remember," the doctor replied.

To Tari he said, "With the great support and friends you obviously have, I'm sure you'll find your way through."

Tari wanted to believe the doctor. She was exhausted and confused on so many levels. According to the doctor over two months of her life were missing and they must have been important months. She was going to have to rely on friends she didn't remember and a fiancé she couldn't even remember dating.

Chapter 14

Even a Queen needs her beauty sleep.

D ragon felt Tari's hand go limp in his and looked down to see her eyes closed. He must have looked as worried as he felt because the doctor quickly reassured him.

"She's just asleep. You should expect her to do that for a little while. Her body has gotten no exercise in the last six days, so even the exam we gave her will have been exhausting."

After watching her unresponsive for so long it was hard to accept that this time she was just asleep. He had her back now and wouldn't let her go. He had to make her safe but he wasn't a doctor, so he had to trust this man knew what he was talking about.

"We still don't know who attacked her. If she doesn't remember, finding the son of a bitch who did this will be difficult." But he knew he would find the man or men responsible and they would pray for death before he was done.

"She may remember but putting pressure on her is likely the worst way to accomplish that. Amnesia like this isn't well understood. It is more than just her short-term memory so there is psychological as well as physiological components. You would do well to find someone for her to talk to not just about the memory loss but to help her adjust. She might experience severe mood swings or even PTSD."

"And the language thing?"

"People who wake from long term comas often have neurological issues. One girl woke up from a coma speaking a different language another had a complete personality change. Hopefully, this is all temporary as her mind readjusts."

Dragon left Val with the sleeping Tari. He wanted to grab food and pick-up Citlali so the little girl could see her mama awake. She was too young to understand what was going on but she knew something was wrong. He strode down the hall to the waiting room to let the Brother on duty there know what was going on before he left.

The sight of Max in his crazy biker glory, sitting across the waiting room from a very nervous looking yuppie family, made Dragon smile. They huddled away from him like he might go feral at any moment. Those close-minded suburbanites would never comprehend the real meaning of family that he and his Brothers lived and breathed every day.

Max was Road Captain for the Dark Sons and one of the most laid-back, chill men he had ever met. Unless he was riding motocross. The man pulled insane tricks that had made him legend in certain circles. Rumor among the Brothers was the man had been a SEAL before getting drawn into blacker ops but he never talked about it and Dragon respected him enough to let his demons rest.

"You look like a man just let out on parole," Max teased. "Heard your woman is awake."

"Awake and now sleeping. Val's sitting with her. I'm grabbing dinner with *mi madre* and *mi hija* then we'll all come back and visit."

Max looked over at the family still giving him wary looks. "Let me take a walk with you." Max didn't say anything until they were outside heading to his bike. "She tell you who attacked her?"

"No. Doctor says she has amnesia. She doesn't remember the last two months."

"Guess that's good and bad news."

"How do you figure?"

"Well, she doesn't remember Didi."

Dragon groaned. "You know I wasn't fucking around with her."

"Yeah but you said you two hadn't worked that shit out so the way I see it you get a fresh start."

He needed a real start with Tari. The unknown threat hanging over their head had to be dealt with and he needed time to show her they were meant to be together.

"You didn't follow me out here just to ask about that."

"No, two things. First, Puck found out something interesting this morning when he was chatting up the receptionist."

Dragon had spent many long hours with Puck when they had been guarding Pixie a few months ago. The man was a classic 'boy next door' handsome and used his good looks to charm as many women as possible out of their panties. He was still a prospect but Dragon guessed it wouldn't be long before he earned his bottom rocker. The fact he had been hitting on a woman while on guard duty came as no surprise.

"What did he learn?"

"Someone's been calling for your woman several times a

day but they always hang up when they hear she can't receive calls."

"You think it might be the man who attacked her."

"Yeah. I already talked to Hawk and he's agreed to station someone here even off hours. They'll have to be in the waiting room but it's the best we can do."

"Shit." Dragon didn't like the thought that Tari's attacker could be actively stalking her. The hospital had security but he doubted it could stop someone determined to kill. "What's the second thing."

"I know you're looking into the problems at the yoga place. Sharp had me use some contacts I have in law enforcement to test the heroine we found stashed there. The mix came back matching some seized from a Jacks distributor."

"Seriously? You thinks those crazy assholes were stupid enough to set up shop in one of our businesses?" Dragon asked, surprised at what he was hearing.

"That's where I think we actually fucked up. Three years ago when Dozer bought that place for Val, Denver narcotics had it pegged already as a possible distributor. I think we actually moved in on them."

That would explain why the books he had been reviewing seemed wrong from day one. The business was always in the black but the numbers were too perfect like someone was always recording just enough business to keep Dozer from looking any closer.

"Why wouldn't they have made problems back then or moved shop?"

"My guess is since Dozer left the staff in place they just saw it as an extra cut out between the product and them."

"Why haven't we heard anything since we shut them down? Even if they didn't realize it was Dark Sons it has been long enough that they should have figured it out." Dragon was amazed that anyone could be that stupid.

"That I don't know. It's not like we are low profile."

Dragon left to meet up with his mother and daughter at a local diner, letting the problems bubble in the back of his mind. He enjoyed watching his daughter babble and laugh with his mother while making a mess of her mac and cheese. When he ordered his burger, he smiled and remembered not to put mustard on it.

Chapter 15

When you hear a southern woman say, "Ohh Hayelll No!" You better bolt.

Tari woke to the sound of Val humming a popular country song just slightly off tune. She felt a lot clearer and was able to raise her hand to brush away a piece of hair from her face. Her fingers and toes all wiggled on command though the soreness in her stomach had turned into a dull ache that was echoed in her head.

"How you feeling, sugar?"

"Sore but good. Where's Dragon?"

"He went to grab dinner then bring your little darlin' back here."

"Oh." She was disappointed he wasn't still there but kicked herself mentally. He would be back. It hadn't been a dream. She tried again to remember how they had reconnected but the place where those memories should be remained out of reach. "Can I ask you a question?"

"Of course."

"Why are you *here*? I know *that sounds rude, but from my memories* you were a student *and I liked you but how did we become friends*?"

Val looked puzzled for a moment. "Darlin', about half of what you just said was in English."

Tari forced herself to focus on each word and by the end Val looked almost hurt.

"I think your memory of our relationship and mine are very different. You have no idea what a blessing you have been in my life. Sure, we didn't chat on the phone but you changed my life."

"Really?"

"Yes. Do you remember the first time we met?"

Tari did. She had just gotten the job as yoga instructor back then the studio had been called The Wellness Spa and was a ratty hole in the wall. She had been on her way to teach a meditation class when she saw a woman hunched over on a bench like she was in pain.

"Of course."

"I didn't tell you then, but I had just received the news that the latest fertility treatment we had tried hadn't worked. I was so lost in my own pain, I didn't know where I was. You sat down next to me and told me to breathe."

Tari laughed because she remembered the dirty look Val had shot her way.

"You said breath was the center of life; it gives our minds and our souls the space and energy they need to heal all wounds and solve all problems. Without enough breath we're paralyzed by the pain. Then you offered me a free class and said it wouldn't fix what was wrong but maybe it would help me learn to breathe."

Tari had always found herself drawn to people who were hurting since she had spent so much of her life getting emotionally battered. Yoga and meditation had given her the strength to get through it all and she wanted others to find that peace with her.

She concentrated on her words as she responded. "I was surprised you came."

"So was I. I'm not exactly a granola loving hippie but your classes weren't about that. After the first month my husband bought the place because he said if something made me so happy it should be nicer."

"You're the one who *bought* the place and gave it a *makeover*?"

"You're still mixing your words, Tari but I think I understood that. Yes, you found that out a week ago when I fired Fifi and Marco when they tried to fire you for bringing Lali to class."

A sharp bolt of pain zipped across Tari's mind as a memory flickered then slipped out of reach.

"You and your classes were a constant source of peace and enjoyment in my life. I was a trauma nurse here at Denver Medical. The things you taught me helped make things not seem so bleak. That night when we went out after class with several other students and everyone was busy bitching about their stress and jobs you said something that changed my life again."

Tari barely remembered the night out she was talking about. Before Citlali going for a drink after the studio closed wasn't an uncommon event. "I don't remember."

"Well I do. You said we all needed to ask ourselves a simple question. Were we working to live or living to work? You said if we were putting up with stress because it was necessary for us to survive then we should see if there was a better way and pull up our big boy pants until we found it. But if we were choosing to live miserable lives for no good reason then we were just masochists and should wake up and enjoy life."

Tari must have had an extra drink that night. She didn't usually have the guts to say things like that. "That changed your life?"

"Sure did. I hated being a trauma nurse. I became a nurse because I like helping people. We didn't need the money or the crazy schedule that goes with that job. I am now a part-time nurse at a VA rehab hospital and I love it. You made that difference. I have always thought of you as a friend." Val laughed. "Dozer came back early with everything going on and him and I are both enjoying living up to your most recent life advice."

Tari wondered what other sage advice she had given. The woman made her sound like she was a wisewoman or something. Before she could ask, they were interrupted.

"Nefertari Johnson?"

The male voice tinged with a slight Northern California accent broke up their conversation. Tari looked over to see a strange man standing in her doorway. He was middle aged with a slight belly and a scowl that could scare children. He had muddy brown hair that was slicked back in an unflattering style and wore a suit that fit him a little too tight. A gun and badge were clipped to his belt. Something about his eyes caused pain to lash across her brain, biting back a whimper she tried to answer him.

"C'est moi." That time Tari realized she had spoken in French. She was starting to get a feel for the fuzziness that was probably the cause of her odd speech. She didn't know that she could control it without effort but it was good to know she might be able to be aware of when it happened.

"What did you say?"

"I'm Tari."

"Ohh. Hayell. No." Val muttered under her breath as she pulled out her phone and fiddled with it.

"I'd like to speak to you alone, please."

Tari didn't like anything about this man, from his tone of voice to his greasy looks. She felt like she knew and disliked him but nothing was coming up when she tried to remember. He was obviously a police officer. Did she have a choice not to talk to him? Focusing on every word she spoke very slowly.

"Who… are… you? What… is… this… about?"

"Why are you talking like that?" His lip curled as he spoke.

Val with her phone to her ear snarled. "Because she just got out of a coma after nearly being beaten to death, you moron. Hey Cheryl, it's Val. You're now on speaker." The sassy southern woman tilted the phone down. "Officer Volker is at Tari's room for some reason, so I thought it good to have you on the line."

Tari didn't think the man's face could get more unpleasant but the sneer he leveled at Val managed the job. "If it isn't one of the criminal's so-called wife."

"Bless your heart officer." Val had a syrupy smile plastered on her face that anyone could tell was fake.

"Please be aware, Officer Volker this conversation is being recorded. I'm Cheryl Lightwin, Ms. Johnson's attorney," a female voice, Tari didn't recognize, said through Val's phone. When had she gotten an attorney? Why did she need an attorney?

Volker looked like he either wanted to smash the phone or the woman holding it. "Why does Ms. Johnson need an attorney? She's the supposed victim."

Supposed victim? Tari didn't remember anything but since she had never committed a crime other than jaywalking, she doubted two months could have turned her into a criminal. Plus, she was the one in the hospital.

"She has the right to an attorney regardless if she is

accused of a crime." Cheryl's voice sounded bored. "Though I am curious why a State Police detective is asking questions of a victim of a crime that happened inside Denver city limits."

"I volunteered to assist the Denver Gang task force. Since I'm familiar with the gang involved."

Tari knew of at least three gangs she saw between where she lived and worked. She wondered which one of them he knew. "You… know… who… attacked me?"

"Oh I am very familiar with the Dark Sons motorcycle gang."

His words confused her. She had heard of the Dark Sons MC, anyone who had lived in Denver had. But everything she had heard about them was mostly good. Sure, they were known for wild parties and probably weren't always on the right side of the law but she had never heard of them being randomly violent. What had she done to get on their bad side?

"*Why would they hurt me?*" Tari tried to say but she could tell by the fuzzy feeling in her mind it had come out wrong.

"What did she just say?" Officer Volker sounded offended.

"I hope she just said you're dumber than a gelding mounting a mare for even suggesting the Dark Sons Motorcycle Club had anything to do with attacking her." Val now looked like she was the one ready to start assaulting someone.

"You call me dumb? She gets engaged to a Dark Sons thug then is beaten into a coma inside a locked apartment. I'm thinking domestic abuse is more likely than a random attack she supposedly can't remember."

He thought Dragon did this to her? Wait, Dragon was a member of the Dark Sons? Val, Volker and the woman on the phone started yelling at each other but Tari's head was pounding so hard she couldn't understand their words. She tried centering herself, breathing deeply, blocking them out.

There were a lot of things she needed to understand but somehow, she knew Dragon wasn't the one who had hurt her body. Focusing on her breathing she found peace within the chaos around her and reached for the nurse's call button and pressed it. The nurse's face when she entered the room was livid. Tari only guessed what she was hearing because she was still blocking the argument out.

Gathering her calm, Tari refocused on the room and pointed at the now purple-faced Officer Volker and said clearly, "I want him out."

The nurse picked up a phone on the wall and Tari could hear her calling for security. Val was smirking as Cheryl's voice came clear from the phone.

"Dragon has already provided proof to the police he was out of the city when the attack occurred. Your slanderous remarks and baiting of a woman only hours after recovering from a coma have been recorded and will be provided to your superiors."

Two men wearing hospital security uniforms rushed into the room right as Volker grabbed Val's phone, and threw it so hard it shattered against the wall. He might have taken a swing at the woman, as well, if one of the security guards hadn't taken him by the arm.

Volker seemed to pull himself together, and started to let security escort him from the room, but not before he took a parting shot.

"Dragon may not be the one who hurt you, but you better remember it has something to do with his gang. I hope you think hard about that, before it is your daughter who gets hurt because you decided to remember the wrong thing."

Tari couldn't help but feel like he was threatening her daughter if she didn't turn against Dragon. Fury rose up in her as she yelled, "*Espero que te quemes en el infierno.*" Burning in Hell wasn't enough of a punishment for someone who threatened her daughter.

Volker left the room along with the two security guards.

Val gave a nervous laugh. "I don't know what you just said, but by the tone, I agree." She straightened her clothing and looked Tari over. "Good call on getting the nurse in here."

Someone cleared their throat and Tari looked to her left. A man was standing in the doorway, a sleek wall of muscle wrapped in jeans, a black t-shirt, and a black leather vest. He had light brown hair and a wild beard. The most remarkable part of him was his vivid, almost aqua-blue eyes which took in the room with calculation.

"She said she hopes he rots in Hell. Are you ladies okay?" Tari found the man's voice almost unnerving because it held no accent. It reminded her of the washed-out tones of a national newscaster. Something that had been trained into him by a vocal coach. She found accents comforting, like a story that told where people were from. Each one unique, explaining pieces of who you were. When they were missing it was like a mystery she wanted to unravel.

Once, when she had been a teen, a man visited the small Eastern European village where her adoptive parents had been missionaries. He had known almost as many languages as she did but had spoken them all with that odd generic accent. He had hidden out among the people asking questions that were a little too pointed. Later, her parents had told her the man had been a spy, though how her parents would have known was a mystery.

If this man was a spy or an ex-spy he would probably know multiple languages. Her ridiculous theory made her smile. What other entertainment did she have? She purposefully answered him in Russian testing the waters. "*We're fine. Who are you, handsome?*"

His lips twitched and a slow smile broke over his face replacing the worried scowl.

"Your languages are getting mixed up again, Sweetie." Val looked concerned. "We're fine Max. Officer Volker was trying to make trouble, but he won't be let back in. Can you call Cheryl and tell her we are okay and let Dozer know I'll need a new phone?"

"Sure thing, Val." He winked at her and looked at Val with a cocky smile. He spoke to Tari in flawless Russian. "*Careful who you flirt with, beautiful.*" Again, his accent was bland and so generic it made her perk up in fascination. Could she really be right?

Tari laughed and for the first time in a long time felt the urge to play. She switched to Mandarin wondering how far his language skills extended. "*I'm engaged to Dragon you white devil. But if I'm ever back in the market for a mysterious man I will let you know.*"

Max's roar of laughter surprised both women. He shook his head and turned around. Tari saw the Dark Sons Denver patch on his back and started to put a few more things together. "Dragon's a lucky man," Max said as he walked out the door.

"What did you say to him?"

Tari focused on English and spoke slowly. It was annoying her brain only seemed to be tripping on English, but she would find a way to compensate. "I called him a white devil."

"Must be funnier in Chinese."

"It is. So, Dragon's a member of the Dark Sons."

"Yes. And so is my husband. I guess you don't remember that. You didn't seem to have a problem with it before. Do you now?"

Did she? As far as she knew she didn't have any firsthand knowledge of the motorcycle club. She had heard plenty of rumors and speculation, and plenty of gushing almost fantasy-like stories from her freshmen year roommate. She understood closed societies more than most having been raised by funda-mentalist Christians who, when not working as missionaries, lived in segregated compounds. But the outlaw motorcycle clubs seemed to represent the opposite of that lifestyle and maybe that added to the appeal.

"I don't think so. Was Officer Volker right? Was I attacked because of my connection to Dragon?"

"Volker is a dirty cop who got busted down in rank a few months ago when someone paid him to put pressure on the Dark Sons and it blew up in his face."

"But could he be right?" Tari didn't know what she would do if it was true but it was better to know. She was glad Val paused to consider and didn't immediately offer an empty platitude.

"I don't see how. Only a handful of people even knew the two of you had a connection before the attack. Plus, Sharp was the one you called when you were hurt. If you thought Dark Sons were the danger you wouldn't have done that."

"Sharp?" Val's words made sense, but without her memory could she be sure?

"Pixie's old man. You knew he was VP of the Dark Sons."

Tari needed time to think. She lived her life trying not to judge others the way her parents had but it was human nature to make generalizations. Personally, she wanted to believe that the MC wasn't bad, but she had Lali to think about. Did she want her daughter to be raised in a group that stood outside the norm of society? Tari needed to act slowly and see what it meant to be part of the Dark Sons world before she could make any real decisions.

Chapter 16

There's always a wild side to an innocent face

Dragon wanted nothing more than to get back in and see how Tari was doing but when Max waved at him from the waiting room, he sent his mother and Lali ahead. Max now had the waiting room to himself; the family from earlier was gone.

"What's up?" Dragon tried not to let his impatience color his voice but from the smirk on Max's face he'd failed.

"Your woman is something else."

Dragon felt a surge of jealousy at the mild comment. "She is." He bit off the possessive words that wanted to follow. "Something I need to know?"

A light twinkled in Max's eye but his Brother seemed to sense the tension and didn't keep pushing. "Officer Volker paid her a visit."

Dragon felt the urge to punch something and right at the moment his Brother's smug face was a tempting target. He had always admired Max but never really connected with him. The Dark Sons' Road Captain was always a little too laid back for Dragon's mind. He acted as if the world was nothing but good times and sweet pussy but something in the man's eyes never quite matched his body language.

"Why did you let that asshole get near her?"

Dragon had never interacted personally with Volker but in the past the officer had been bought and paid for by sex traffickers which was one of many reasons not to trust him around women. He had even tried to get his hands on Pixie so he could give her back to her abuser. There was no way Dragon ever wanted Tari to have to deal with that dirtbag.

"He must have come in through the back way. I didn't know he was here till I saw security running down the hall."

"Shit." Dragon paced imagining every way that could have gone wrong. "There is no way we can protect Tari when there are other ways to get to her room and we are stuck in here."

"That's taken care of. I talked to security and the head nurse for the floor. Explained that she is in danger. They've agreed to let someone sit right outside the room as long as they stay quiet and don't disturb anyone."

Dragon took a deep breath as he felt the stress he had been feeling the last week ease a bit. "I owe you."

"You're family and she's yours. She going to be your Old Lady?"

"Yeah. I let Hawk know last night."

Dragon had seen the President a few times over the last week when he stopped by to check on him. Hawk was a scary son of a bitch whom he was proud to call his Brother. The man had promised him anything he would need to sort out shit with his woman and the crap with Dark Zen.

"She know that yet?"

"Not yet."

Max chuckled and shook his head. "We're having Church late tonight so you can stay with your woman for a while, but we need a report on everything you found about Dark Zen's books."

Val strode into the waiting room. "Hey boys, I'm taking off but wanted to talk to you for a moment."

His Brother Dozer had scored high when he snagged this woman who was the heart and soul of the Dark Sons' Old Ladies. She was gorgeous with a rocking body that was always shown off to perfection in glittering skin-tight outfits. Dragon might not be attracted to the big red hair and southern rhinestone style the woman rocked but he could appreciate her big heart and generous nature.

"What did you need?" Max asked.

"I'm sure Cheryl already sent the tape to Hawk of what Volker said to Tari, but I just can't shake the idea the man knows something we don't, about what happened to Tari."

"You think he had something to do with it?" Dragon would happily end that man's existence if he had laid a finger on Tari.

"The man's a hyena, not a wolf, so I don't figure he was there. I would say he knows who it was though. After he smashed my phone, he warned that Tari remembering the wrong thing might be dangerous. Said it might be Lali that got hurt next time."

"*Hijo de puta!*" Threatening a one-year-old was depravity on a level he couldn't accept. Keeping his daughter safe was too important not to act and soon. Dragon was going to end that man one way or another.

Chapter 17

Girl, speak up. You'll never know unless you ask

T ari marveled at the Hispanic woman who was making her daughter giggle like she was having the time of her life. Her name was Itzli but she insisted on being called Mama Rios. Dragon's mother was a small, curvy woman with the same sharp regal features in her face that her son had. How the tiny woman had given birth to the giant of a man was a mystery.

She was maybe in her early fifties but had an ageless strength about her that Tari admired. As soon as she realized Tari spoke Spanish, she had been regaling her with crazy tales of Dragon and his sister when they were children. It was good she was willing to hold up most of the conversation because Tari was trying to adjust to how big her little girl looked.

Two months made a lot of difference in her Lali and it was hard to wrap her brain around the fact somewhere in that missing time she had gained so many friends and family.

"So, when are you and Gabor going to give me more grandbabies to spoil?"

Tari laughed. *"One isn't enough?"*

"Oh my goodness no. A woman needs many babies around to love. My daughter has two, but I want to fill my house with more grandbabies."

"Mama you will scare her away. Then how many grandchildren will you have?" Dragon leaned down and kissed his mother on the cheek then did the same to their daughter.

"Papa up!" Lali demanded and Tari had to fight back happy tears as Dragon swung their little girl up and around in a circle causing her to giggle in delight.

Her man might be a 6'6" tattooed badass but the sight of him swirling their little girl in his arms was something she would always remember. He tickled her tummy and blew raspberries on her cheeks like he played with toddlers every day of his life. He was wearing what she liked to think of as the biker uniform of combat boots, worn jeans, tight black t-shirt and a leather vest. Or was it called a cut? Either way, the faded black leather matched the one Max had been wearing earlier in most ways, but had different patches on the front. She wondered what those differences meant.

Lali squealed in delight as Dragon gave her a small toss into the air. His eyes were practically glowing with the love he so obviously felt for the little girl making him somehow even more gorgeous. Tari wished she could remember what Dragon's reaction had been when she told him about Citlali, but she couldn't even dig up a flicker of memory.

Seeing Dragon standing there perfect in so many ways, Tari was glad the nurse had come in earlier to remove the worst of the medical equipment and help her clean up. She had even been able to change out of the embarrassing hospital gown into a pair of yoga pants and large Harley shirt that Val had brought in for her. If she was careful not to move or pull any stitches, she could almost pretend the four of them weren't sitting in a gloomy hospital.

"*How is my queen doing?*" Dragon asked in Spanish as he leaned down and brushed a kiss across her lips. His touch was magic, sending sparks of pleasure with just that small contact. Lali grabbed a piece of Tari's hair and pulled a little too hard.

Pain spiked as the action pulled the stitches in Tari's scalp and she hissed out a breath. Dragon apologized and quickly got the little girl's hands untangled.

Tari breathed, slowly pushing away the pain and then managing a smile. "*I'm fine. The nurse said that all my stitches will come out tomorrow. If all goes well, I can go home the next day.*" The nurse had said her body was healing remarkably fast, but her mind was still uncertain. It bothered her that the only way she could talk without problems was in another language. That wouldn't work for most people.

"Isn't that too soon?" Dragon looked concerned.

"*They are only keeping me that long to be sure I've recovered from the coma.*"

"*Don't you worry, son. I will stay with her and that lovely Val is a nurse. She will be fine.*" Mama Rios patted Dragon on the arm. "I *will leave you two lovebirds alone and get the little princess home to sleep.*"

Tari hated to see her daughter go but it was getting late and she needed to ask Dragon some questions before he had to leave when visiting hours were over. With kisses and promises to visit tomorrow Tari said goodbye to her daughter and the woman who was going to be her mother-in-law.

"Puck will escort you back to my place, Mama, he's waiting downstairs." Fear shot down Tari's spine as Dragon gave a final kiss to his mother and daughter. Where did Dragon live? Was the place childproofed? Did he live in the city or suburbs? Thousands of questions bubbled up but they boiled down to a single question.

"Is your place safe?"

"Yes, *Mami*." A thrill of something other than fear filled her at his use of the Spanish endearment. "I live at the Club compound; there isn't a safer place for them."

Tari wasn't sure she liked the idea of living in another compound but pushed the thought away for another day. This was her first opportunity to be alone with Dragon that she remembered. Everything since she woke up felt like she was living a weird but wonderful version of the life she remembered. Her solitary existence had been turned upside down and she knew it had everything to do with the wonderful man now smiling at her with hungry eyes.

"You are so beautiful, *mi reina*."

Tari shook her head. She had taken time to look at herself in the mirror. Her right eye was still swollen, and bruising was visible along her jaw. She had managed to untangle the mess that was her hair but the line of stitches that ran from the bottom of her throat, between her breasts, to her abdomen was clearly visible. That didn't count the Frankenstein horror show that was her stomach or the shaved patch at the base of her skull where they had drilled a hole.

"You doubt me?"

"I looked in a mirror."

He came over and sat on the bed. Tari normally would love the way his big body made her feel like she was small, but pain and uncertainty made her wish he was a little less tall.

"You will always be the most beautiful woman in the world to me." He took her hand in his and kissed her knuckles sending pleasant shivers up her arm.

His action reminded her of a question she had been pondering. "How did we get engaged? Actually, how did you find me? I know I'm missing two months but it is like I've missed years instead."

Dragon looked like he was torn. He looked away from her gaze and Tari got a sinking feeling he was going to avoid the question. What could be so bad that he didn't want to tell her? Had he only proposed because of Lali? Was she misreading everything?

"Tell me the truth. I need to know."

He cleared his throat. "You found me, or I guess, really you told Val and Pixie about me and they made the connection."

A sharp sting of memory flashed across her mind. A restaurant and Pixie showing her a photo. As quickly as it came it slipped away.

"Our first meeting didn't go well and our second wasn't much better. Misunderstandings happened and I tried to move too fast. I didn't know about our daughter. I was so happy to see you again after so long I tried to pick up right where we left off."

Since they had left off sweaty and satisfied in a motel room Tari could only imagine what that meant.

"Well, I guess we worked through that since you asked me to marry you, and I said yes." Had he only proposed because of their daughter? Tari didn't think she would have said yes if that was the case. Lali should have her father in her life but that would be tainted if he was stuck in a marriage he didn't want.

"We're not exactly engaged."

"What does not exactly mean? The nurse called you my fiancé and your mama…"

"You were hurt later that night on the same day you contacted me. You hadn't yet told me about our daughter. When Puck found you unconscious, Lali was with you. Val took care of her till I got here and told me everything. We lied to the hospital so they would tell us what was going on."

Her daughter's cries echoed in her mind as phantom pain tore through her stomach. She tried to form words, but they just wouldn't come. She breathed deeply focusing her energy centering herself.

"You okay, Tari? Should I get the nurse?"

She shook her head slightly afraid of losing her control if she moved too much. Random ideas ping-ponged through her mind. Relief that it couldn't be Dragon's fault that she was here. Confusion over the connection between the two of them. Without months of forgotten history between them it didn't make sense.

"So, we are nothing to each other?" Each word was hard won but she knew she got each one out clearly.

"Don't say that, *querida*. Never say that. You are special to me. The mother of my child and the woman who sets my pulse racing with a thought."

"Dragon, I would never keep your daughter from you. You don't have to pretend."

He leaned in and kissed her lips, gentle at first, but his tongue swept out demanding entry. Tari gasped, and he took advantage, claiming her mouth with his. Fire ignited deep inside her and all the pain and confusion melted away. Memories of pleasure echoed through her body like phantom hands and she could almost feel him deep in her core echoing the motions of his tongue.

"Does this feel like pretend?" He took her hand and placed it on his lap.

She could feel the long, hard length of him through his jeans. She rubbed along the bulge and felt his cock jump against her palm.

"No."

"I dream of your voice, your laugh. I sometimes imagine I

can still taste you on my tongue. I've been building a list of all the things I want to do with your gorgeous body and when you're better, I intend to go through every last one of them." Her hand and her pussy clenched at his words and she could almost wish he would start right now. He gripped her wrist stilling her hand. "If you don't stop that I am going to be coming in my pants like a teenage boy."

She licked her lips wishing she could suck him off but knowing she wasn't there yet. A naughty thought crossed her mind and she closed her eyes shivering as she pictured it.

"What was that thought that has your nipples so hard I can see them through your shirt?"

Her pussy clenched and her stomach twitched sending tiny shocks of pain and pleasure through her system.

"Nothing." She blushed, embarrassed by her own thoughts. Here she was lying in a bed looking like hell imagining her hot, sort of boyfriend doing sexual things to himself.

He lifted her chin till their gazes locked. "That wasn't nothing, *Mami*. I think you have something you want me to add to that list." His grin was absolutely wicked and his heated words gave her courage.

"No, *Papi*. It's something I want you to do now."

Sparkling fire seemed to leap from his eyes, but it gentled. "I would love to do wicked things to your body but I don't want to hurt you."

"*Not to me. I want to watch you touch yourself while you look at me. I want to see you come while I think about how wonderful it will feel when you can finally sink deep inside me.*" She bit her lip wondering if she had asked too much. She had slipped back into Spanish wanting to be sure he knew what she wanted.

He growled low and stood up. Tari thought she had lost him as he strode over to the bathroom, looked around, and for some reason grabbed a washcloth. A sexy smirk played at his lips as he paused in the doorway to the bathroom and leaned against the doorframe.

Standing there framed in the doorway he was like a piece of dark artwork. Anyone coming in the main door wouldn't immediately be able to see him because of the curtain, but she had the perfect front on view. He opened his zipper and Tari moaned at the beautiful sight as he pulled out his cock. She had remembered he was big but the in person visual made her wish she could jump out of bed and join him.

He took several slow strokes twisting his wrist as he reached the head. She only wished she could see the wonderful muscles of his chest. Surely after two years he still had that luscious V that had played a starring role in her masturbation fantasies.

"Is this what you want, *Mami?* You want to see my cock as I fantasize about the feeling of your tight pussy wrapped around me."

"Yes." Her breathing sped up as she watched him stroking the length of himself. She could almost feel it inside her. She imagined herself down on her knees tasting the salt of his sweat as he pushed in and out of her mouth. The soft velvet over steel feel of his cock gliding over her tongue.

"I want to spend hours claiming every part of that gorgeous body, till you have trouble remembering what your body feels like without me in it." His strokes sped up and Tari could see his muscles flexing under his shirt.

His voice became breathy and Tari swore she could see his hand straining as it roughly moved up and down. "First, I'm going to fuck that sweet mouth while you ride my face until you're screaming from orgasm."

Tari clenched her hands in the sheets, her panting breaths now matching his rhythm.

"Then I'm going to fuck you so hard and deep you'll feel me in your womb. And when you're boneless from coming so hard you don't think you can move, I'm going to fuck your tight ass and make you come one… last... time."

Tari's body spasmed and she swore she came right along with him even though she hadn't been touching herself. Dragon had brought the washcloth down as his face contorted with ecstasy, catching his release. Tari wished he hadn't thought to use the towel because her mind filled in the image of her body covered in his cum.

A knock on the door broke them both out of the breathless haze they had entered.

"Visiting hours are over." A pleasant voice called through the door.

Dragon stepped back, tossing the towel in the sink and tucking his cock into his jeans. A teasing smile lit his face as he zipped up. He strode over to the bed and captured her lips in a passionate kiss. Tari was completely breathless when he finally pulled away.

"Oh, that is definitely going on my list, *Mami* along with any other dirty fantasies you have."

Chapter 18

Stay real. Stay loyal or stay the fuck away from me.

R iding back to the compound was one of the hardest things Dragon had ever done. Tari was awake and, even though he knew she had protection, he wanted to be the one at her side. They had a long hard road ahead of them and, until he knew the men who had attacked her were permanently gone from this earth, he didn't believe they could start down it.

The doctor had warned him Tari would probably have physical and emotional issues on top of the language ones she already faced. He didn't care. He would find the money to get her the best therapists Denver had to offer. The language thing was scary but she did fine in Spanish so they already had a way around that. If she had trouble walking, then he would carry her everywhere she needed to go.

All that mattered was she and their daughter were safe and happy. He pulled up to the Clubhouse and saw, by the number of motorcycles out front, most of the Brothers were already there. Knowing he was holding up the meeting, Dragon didn't waste any more time.

The Dark Sons Clubhouse was a large, two-story building that was set up specifically for them. The first story had a large open space which held a bar, pool tables, and enough seating and tables that even when all the Brothers and the hangers-on were present it didn't feel small. A huge industrial kitchen took up most of the back of the building along with offices for the officers. Off to the side was the meeting room where they held Church. The second floor had another lounge and several bedrooms that Brothers would use to crash or take women up to when they didn't want to go home.

The basement was completely open and mostly contained workout equipment and training mats; the Brothers often sparred there to keep up their skills. The entire compound was designed with the idea that if trouble ever came knocking, all the Brothers and their families could live and be safe for a time with high-tech security and everything a large group of people needed. The outlaw lifestyle wasn't for everyone, but Dragon felt peaceful knowing he belonged to something bigger than himself.

When Dragon stepped inside the building, he saw Puck behind the bar serving drinks. The week had been so crazy he hadn't had time to speak to him and thank him for getting Tari to the hospital in time.

"Hey Dragon, want a beer?" Puck offered up an open bottle that Dragon gladly accepted.

"I haven't gotten a chance to thank you for what you did for Tari."

"No problem. That was some intense shit. How is she doing?"

"Better. She woke up today. Has memory loss and some

other issues but she's alive. I won't ever forget how much I owe you."

Dragon could almost see a blush on the pretty boy Prospect's cheeks as he shook his head. A punch landed on his shoulder and Dragon turned to see Hawk grinning at him. The President of the Dark Sons was in his early forties with black hair peppered with gray. His body was still in prime condition and was known for his brutal sparring sessions that often left his opponents groaning on the mat. Between him and Sharp, Dragon couldn't have asked for stronger leaders who were ruthlessly loyal to the men under them.

"About time you got here." Hawk's words were friendly. "Stop messing with the Prospect, it's time for Church."

A few of his Brothers asked after his woman and Dragon was glad she had so many good men worrying after her. The beginning of the meeting was the usual boring things that had to be dealt with in a large organization. They had a charity run coming up in two weeks and they were doing several protection runs for the Minetti family which Dragon wouldn't be participating in because he had a pass till the business with Tari was resolved.

Dozer ran his hand through his hair. "That leaves the Dark Zen mess. Max and Dragon have the Intel on that."

Max leaned back in his chair at the officers table looking, as always, like he didn't have a care in the world. "I've managed to confirm the Jacks have been using the location as one of their main distribution points for heroin for over seven years. Marco, the manager, was one of their upper member's brother."

"Was?" Sharp asked from his end of the table.

"Yeah, was. He was found beaten to death in his place last night. Fifi, who apparently wasn't really Marco's wife, has been missing since the day you fired her."

"You think she's still alive?" Hawk asked.

Max shrugged. "The Jacks aren't known for being subtle so I think if she was dead, we would know it. What troubles me more is we got rid of over 100k of their product that was stored in the back room of Dark Zen. They haven't done or said shit about wanting it back."

Hawk leaned forward, his angry face enough to give anyone pause. "Everyone knows we don't deal in drugs and we don't shit in our own backyard. They had the balls to keep using the location even after we bought it. Maybe they think if they keep quiet, we won't figure it out."

Dragon was sure there was more going on than just fear of war. Dark Sons had the Jacks outnumbered, outgunned, and definitely outclassed but the street thugs lived on their reputation. If it became known they had been punked by the MC they would be forced to react.

"I think there is something we're missing." Dragon felt the puzzle pieces moving in his mind but they weren't lining up. "From what I can tell, from the books, the only thing slightly correct in the numbers is payroll. Even there I can't believe we have kept even a single employee at the rates listed. It's like someone found the perfect numbers to pacify the IRS then doctored the income to show exactly a five-percent profit every month to keep us from looking closer. No business is that perfect."

"You think it is more than the drugs?" Dozer growled.

"Yeah. Turns out there are files on fifty-three employees in a shop that maybe should have fifteen at the high end. One area for exercise and four spa rooms. We only knew about six of them and those are the only employees who log more than five hours a week. Two of those were the piece of shit management team we fired."

Hawk sat back and crossed his arms. "Prostitution?"

Dragon nodded. "Men and women if what I am seeing is right; and too many of the tax ID numbers I found are for kids under eighteen. Their files listed them as personal trainer assistants."

Sharp cursed and muttered arguments broke out throughout the room. Dark Sons had a few strip clubs they ran where the services of the women extended to more than just dancing but they were very careful that their girls were clean, protected, and, most importantly, of age. They did not deal with drugs or underage anything, yet somehow the Jacks had used their business to cover up both.

"Highdive." Hawk barked the Enforcer's name and the room settled down. "Get the names of the employees and interview each one of them. Find out what they know about what really happened there. Offer our protection to any you think worth saving. Max, setup a meet with the Jacks' leader Diablo. Make sure he understands I am less than happy about this shit."

"We push them, Hawk and it will be war," Max warned but didn't seem overly concerned.

"They want war, we'll do the people of Denver a favor and make it quick. I don't like fucking with street punks, too much like kicking puppies. But these dogs have been shitting on our lawn. We let it ride and the bigger gangs will think it's open season. Dragon, I know you got your hands full, but have Dozer send you over the financials on the rest of our businesses. Make sure we haven't let any other things sneak up on us."

Tek, the Club's Secretary and the only outlaw biker Dragon knew who was also a billionaire, spoke up, "Send me all the socials I'll have my people see if they can spot any other patterns." Tek was the owner and CEO of the largest security and technology company in Colorado. He never hesitated to help out especially when kids were involved.

Hawk banged his gavel. "All right with that handled, everyone should be on high alert. This thing will probably cause blow-back in the next few weeks. If it gets too hot, I want everything in place for a full lockdown." All heads nodded in agreement. The nice part of most of the Brothers being ex or current military was not a single man ever balked when shit hit the fan. "On a better subject, Max has something to put forward."

Max nodded, giving a real smile. "I want to put forward Puck for patching in. He's been prospecting for only nine months, and while we usually wait a year, his dedication when protecting Pixie and more recently, his quick thinking that saved Dragon's woman and child make for special circumstances. His loyalty is beyond question."

"Anyone have anything to say against him?" Hawk asked the room.

"Nine months is a pussy amount of time. And who the fuck is going to clean my bike as good as he does?" Highdive, the Enforcer and Sergeant at arms, threw out as a joke that had most of the room chuckling.

When Hawk called the vote, as it had to be, Puck was unanimously voted in. Highdive opened the door and all the Brothers put on their best game faces.

"Get that fucker in here!" Hawk bellowed; Dragon was sure everyone in the Clubhouse heard the command.

Highdive and Max ran out and quickly returned dragging a startled Puck between them. They brought him up to the line painted on the ground that marked where only Brothers were allowed to step. Hawk and all the officers now stood in a line five feet on the other side of that divide their arms crossed.

"What the hell?" Puck was flustered but he stood up, body clenched as if expecting a fight.

"You fucking loyal to the Dark Sons?" Hawk barked.

"Yeah. What's this—"

"You willing to live or die for your Brothers?" Sharp broke in with his question.

"Yes." Puck looked around.

"You ride with us, party with us, and keep Dark Sons' business tight?" Max asked.

"Always." Puck relaxed a slight bit.

"What's our creed?" Highdive asked.

"Brothers first. Brothers Forever." Puck stood straighter.

"I make you my Brother. I make you my family. You willing to do everything it takes to protect that family?" Dozer said in a tone that would make a drill sergeant proud.

"Yes Sir." Dragon couldn't help but chuckle at the Sir that was probably a reflex in every man here.

Tek stepped forward holding up the bottom rocker patch that would mark Puck's transition from Prospect to Brother. "You step over that line, take this patch there is no way out but feet first. Decide."

There was no hesitation in Puck's step as Dragon watched him stride forward and take the patch from Tek's hands. As was tradition, all the men rushed him at that point and they lifted him off the ground, carrying him out into the Clubhouse and dumping him on the couch in the middle of the floor. The sweetbutts and female hangers-on who had been waiting for the meeting to break up all swarmed the new Brother wanting to show their support.

Dragon tried to enjoy it: the booze, the women, the celebration for the man who had Prospected with him, but none of it was appealing with his own woman still in the hospital. He took a pull from his beer and pushed away yet another woman who tried to slide up next to him.

"So, she's the one." Tek slid in next to him and signaled Flak for a beer.

"Yup." Dragon raised an eyebrow. "You going to give me shit?"

"Nope. Barely know her but I know you. You're a lucky bastard." Tek accepted a bottle from the Prospect behind the bar and took a long swallow.

"I'm sure there is a woman out there who would be happy to pin your ass down."

Tek gave a bark of laughter. "Oh plenty of women would love to pin down my bank account."

"None of the women here give a shit about that."

"I need a woman smart enough to keep my brain engaged, twisted enough to keep my dick interested, and strong enough to go toe to toe with both the Brotherhood and my boardroom. You find that unicorn you let me know." Tek raised his bottle in a toast and Dragon matched it.

Tari was the strongest woman he knew, but looking around the wild and unconventional Clubhouse, he knew he was going to have a long road to prove to her just how perfect this life was for all of them.

Chapter 19

Learning is a gift and Pain is your teacher.

Tari thought she knew what hell was, but today she was learning a new definition of the word. The morning had started with a cranky nurse who found, to her chagrin, her patient spoke Russian and understood all the insults the woman had been muttering while she removed the hundreds of stitches from her body. The encounter ended up with the two of them hurling insults at each other. A second nurse had to be brought in to finish up.

Then she had to sit through being treated like a rare oddity while a psychiatrist and a gaggle of students ran her through a series of tests that only confirmed what she already knew. The injury to her brain had led to memory loss and linguistic issues when she tried to speak English. But the physical therapist's evaluation was what had her ready to pass out and give up.

Tari had always thought of herself as being in peak physical condition. That had waned a little when she had Lali since she couldn't run anymore, but she taught yoga or Pilates six times a week and worked out with what little she could at home. Now she found herself shaking like a leaf after just a few minutes of nothing more strenuous than walking. Her fine motor skills were such that she couldn't even write legibly.

The therapist was optimistic that with months of physical therapy she would probably fully recover but didn't seem to understand the depth of loss she was feeling. How would she support herself and her daughter if she couldn't work? She had no idea how she was going to pay for this hospital stay.

She tried to be optimistic, the wounds to her stomach could have been so much worse. A plastic surgeon had said most of them wouldn't scar. The scars on the back of her neck would fade with time and could be covered by her hair. She was alive.

Her optimism faded as a headache sliced through her skull and brought her to tears as the nurse finally wheeled her back to her room in the late afternoon. A light skinned black man sat at the entrance to her room wearing what she had come to think of as the Dark Sons uniform: a black t-shirt and jeans with a faded vest covered in patches. The name on the leather was Hannibal which is the only thing that seemed legible to her. Something about him was familiar but the pounding in her head meant she didn't think about it too long.

The nurse got her settled in bed and gave her painkillers. Her mind was soon fuzzy and the fatigue of the day was catching up to her. The large man from outside had moved to the chair in the corner of the room.

"Hannibal?"

He stood up and Tari could now see his skin was covered in gorgeous tattoos. "You need something *cher?*"

It was hard to focus around the drugs and weariness she felt but she did her best. "No visitors *today*." She swallowed around the depression that was threatening to bring her to tears. "I need *time* to think. Tomorrow. I will talk to Dragon *tomorrow*."

She wasn't sure if all her words came out right but Hannibal nodded as if he understood. "I will let them know. Dragon was here all morning. I think he planned on bringing your daughter back."

Tari shook her head. She couldn't face her little girl right now knowing she couldn't be the mother she needed to be. What little stability the little girl had known was about to be thrown into chaos because she wasn't strong enough.

"All right, I'll give him a call. You just sleep, okay?"

Tari liked the soft cadence of his words. His voice held a slight accent from Louisiana somewhere outside New Orleans more country than city. She let his assurances relax her and she fell into dreams.

She was early to yoga class for once and she was enjoying the time to relax in one of the currently unused spa rooms. Her life was so hectic that true moments of quiet were hard to find. She had just started to find her center when sounds came too clearly from the room next door.

"You want your bonus don't you, baby? That's right take it all."

Tari couldn't resist walking towards the wall. Karen, one of the few other employees she liked here, who did facials and massages had told her there were peepholes between the rooms for 'employee safety'. They had both known it was a crock of shit but laughed it off because if watching someone get a massage got their bosses off who were they to complain.

What Tari saw when she looked through the hole had her stifling a giggle. Marco had a girl on her knees, his flabby ass thrusting enthusiastically. From her vantage point, she could see the bored, almost comical, expression on the girl's face as his dick went in and out from her lips that weren't even straining to surround what had to be the seriously unimpressive size of his dick.

"That's right, you take every inch of me. Fuck yeah!"

Well, at least Marco was enjoying himself. Her slimy manager had tried on several occasions to see if Tari was interested in earning bonuses. She had been warned early what that meant and never fell for the line or the one to work after hours in personal sessions. She might love working as a yoga instructor, but she was not even remotely interested in the other services, and hoped she never got desperate enough to consider it.

A hand ran strong fingers up her leg sending chills right up her spine.

"What you looking at, Tari?" Dragon's voice made her relax and she pushed back into his body. She loved feeling him pressing against her back and his hands roaming over the front of her in teasing, feather-light caresses.

What was Dragon doing at her work? How did his touch seem to be everywhere at once? She shook off the confusing thoughts and just lost herself, enjoying the feeling of him all around her.

"Nothing good."

"Do you like looking?"

She blushed at the thought of Dragon learning one of her naughty fantasies. "If it's worth watching." Which the scene in the other room definitely wasn't.

"Look again."

Dragon's hand was between her thighs, and her pants were gone giving him free access to her body. She leaned forward, looking through the hole, the scene behind it completely different. She felt Dragon's fingers slowly slide into her as she saw instead Hannibal sitting watching a blonde woman slowly pleasure herself. The woman was more fake than real, her proportions rivaling the plastic dolls little girls dressed up. But unlike the woman from before, this one seemed to be really enjoying herself.

Dragon's hands started mimicking the woman's, teasing Tari right to the edge and working her back down. The wall melted away and she found herself with an unobstructed view of the room which had now turned into a tattoo parlor. Hannibal's eyes had filled with a dark heat as he watched the woman slide her fingers into her pussy.

Tari felt fingers sliding into her own depths and knew an orgasm was just moments away. The woman moved and Tari could clearly see the man *face down on the tattoo chair in front of Hannibal was Dragon. If Dragon was there who was holding her?*

She screamed, trying to struggle against the hands that held her, and she was lying flat on her back in a dirty alley. Her daughter's screams echoed her own making her pulse race. A dark shape moved towards her daughter while her attacker's face came into focus.

Chapter 20

Your dreams tell me what a wonderful, creative person you are. Your nightmares let me know who it is I have to kill.

Dragon watched Tari sleep from a chair in the corner of her hospital room, worry sending acid up his throat. Why had she told Hannibal to tell him to stay away? He had thought they had left things in a good place. It had been frustrating not being able to see her all day but he'd understood the hospital was trying to make sure she was okay before releasing her.

The conversations with the doctors had made everything seem so upbeat, but according to Hannibal, his girl had looked like she had just received a death sentence. Physically she was in much better shape than they could have hoped with almost full mobility. The tests had shown no further bleeding or damage to her brain. Only time would tell if the neurological issues were permanent but her doctor had no problem releasing her as long as she had someone at home to keep an eye on her.

They had suggested she might want to go to a rehab hospital, but if she did outpatient physical therapy every day it wasn't necessary. Tari would be much safer at the compound and Dragon would take her to each and every appointment for as long as was needed.

Tari thrashed in her sleep and Dragon was immediately at her side brushing her hair out of her face. Her scream of terror sent ice through his veins; her arm shot out clocking him right on the temple and sent him stepping back a pace.

"No, Chobo! Don't hurt my baby please!"

Dragon stepped back to the bed, pinning her arms down, and shaking her as gently as he could with her thrashing.

"Wake up, Tari. It's just a dream. Wake up for me."

A nurse and Grinder rushed in the room both trying to take in what was happening.

"No, Chobo, *please don't.*" Dragon gave her a firm shake and Tari's eyes fluttered open. She looked around, her body slowly relaxing as she pulled out of the nightmare. "Dragon?"

"Yeah, it's me. Who's Chobo?"

Terror filled her eyes. "He's going to hurt Lali." She shook her head. "N*o siento.* I don't… it was only a *rêve.*" She closed her eyes, her breath slowing, but her body wasn't relaxing so he knew she wasn't falling back to sleep. "A dream?" She opened her eyes and her look begged him to tell her it wasn't real.

Dragon looked over to Grinder who just nodded and left the room. The nurse pushed between the two of them and started checking Tari's vitals while almost cooing platitudes about nightmares being understandable and the 'body's way of coping with stress'.

When the woman was finally satisfied that everything was

okay, she left and Dragon sat at the edge of the bed and held Tari's hand.

"What do you remember?"

"*It started out as a memory from a few months ago. I had accidentally seen Marco getting a blowjob from one of the girls at Zen.*" Dragon didn't think she realized she was speaking Spanish but didn't want to interrupt the story. Her face took on a look of horror. "*Dark Sons run prostitutes?*"

Dragon almost got whiplash from how quickly her mind switched topics. "What does this have to do with your dream?"

She blushed. "*I'm not a whore.*"

"I never thought you were."

"*You know I work for Dark Zen. I understand why some women choose to offer more personal services but I wanted you to know I just taught yoga.*"

Understanding hit him and it made him feel shame. Tari had been a single mom struggling to raise his daughter alone. She had two jobs, one of them in a diner one step away from offering 'extras' to the customers. How much easier would it have been for her to make better money on her back?

"No, I never thought that. Whatever was going on at Dark Zen we didn't know about it. Dozer really thought it was just a girlie spa till last week."

The look on Tari's face clearly stated she had a problem believing him. He couldn't lie to her and say Dark Sons didn't deal with prostitutes but he didn't want to argue technicalities either.

"I swear. Before last week we thought everything about that place was legal."

Tari seemed to accept that with a nod. "*My dream got weird after that, you and Hannibal were there and some blow-up blonde.*" Dragon held his breath ready to defend himself if she asked about the scene at the tattoo parlor. "*Then I was in an alley and a man was attacking me and Lali.*"

"Chobo?"

"I think so, but I don't know anyone with that name." Tari shrugged. *"Then I woke up."*

Dragon ran his thumb over her knuckles and prayed Grinder was finding out right now who this Chobo was. The name was unique enough that it gave him hope. The two of them sat in silence for a few minutes, the adrenaline slowly leaving their bodies. When the silence grew uncomfortable Dragon decided to ask what had been bothering him since he had shown up.

"Why did you tell Hannibal I shouldn't come?"

Tari turned her face away and shook her head. The beautiful, black silk of her hair slid down, covering her face.

"*Mi reina* talk to me."

"I am not a queen." Her words were shaky and bitten off. When she continued in Spanish her voice was so choked with emotion, Dragon felt his heart breaking. *"I am barely a woman. They will release me tomorrow and I don't even know if I will still have a place to live. I can't work and if I somehow find a way to do the physical therapy it will be weeks before I might, if I'm really lucky, be able to do a shift as a waitress. How can I keep Lali safe if I can't even pick her up?"*

Dragon pulled Tari into his arms and felt her tears soaking into his shirt hoping he wasn't hurting her but knowing she needed him close.

"You are *una reina*, my queen. Your and Lali's things have been moved to the compound. The only thing you have to worry about is getting better. You're not alone anymore, Tari. I will protect my girls. We will figure everything out." He lifted her chin and met her watery onyx eyes. "I promise. Before you know it you and *mi princesa* will be spoiled."

Dragon wished he saw belief in Tari's eyes but she was too scared for that. He did at least see a slow acceptance growing there.

"*I envy you.*"

"What?"

"*Your mama. What you seem to have with your Brothers. It has been just me and Citlali for so long.*"

"Do you want me to call your parents?"

Tari snorted. "*I don't have parents anymore.*"

Dragon let her lie back stroking her face. "I'm sorry I didn't know they–"

"*Oh, they're not dead.*" She cut him off with a wave of her hand. "*They disowned me when they found out about Citlali.*"

Disbelief hit him in the chest like a blow. He remembered her not talking fondly of her parents' goals for her but this went way beyond that. "Are you fucking kidding me?"

Tari shrugged and winced. "*They are good people in their minds. They adopted me as a baby because my mother died while they were ministering to her not because they actually wanted a child. The world is black and white, there is good and evil. To them what I did with you was evil.*"

She shivered and Dragon wanted to rip apart the people who had hurt his woman like that. He tried to remember what she had said about them in the past but it wasn't much. They were religious missionaries. A horrible thought occurred to him.

"What did they do to you?" Dragon knew there was fury lacing his tone. If they had beaten or harmed them in any way, they would feel the same back tenfold.

"They didn't physically hurt me." She patted his hand. "That was never their way. I was shunned. Which in the community I grew up in was the final and ultimate punishment. In all things that matter, I am dead to them." Tari closed her eyes, but Dragon could still see the hurt on her face. "I don't think they wanted proof of their own failure to raise me right lingering around, casting doubt on their own perfect piety."

"You aren't a failure, and if they can't see that, fuck them." He gave her arm a little shake. Tari opened her eyes and Dragon tried to show her with every part of his body that he meant every word. "You are *my* family now. You and our gorgeous little girl. My family is *yours* now. You have a doting mother, a troublemaking little sister, two nephews, and more Dark Son Brothers than you will know what to do with."

Tears shimmered in her eyes as he leaned in to kiss her. He could only hope she believed him; determined to fulfil every promise he had made and more. "You don't have to worry about them or anyone else." He might not hunt down her parents but he would find Chobo and make him pay for every injury on her body with interest.

Chapter 21

So far you've survived 100% of your worst days.

Tari woke up feeling much better than she had the day before. It wasn't just her body, though removing the stitches had done wonders for not feeling unexpected sharp pain. Mentally she felt rested and like she could face the problems ahead. She was able to take a shower though the nurse made her sit down on a bench. When she got dressed in clean comfy yoga pants and a big t-shirt, Tari almost felt normal.

"Hey beautiful, you ready to blow this joint?" Max said with a teasing tone.

She smiled when Dragon scowled at his Brother, finding the small display of jealousy comforting. "Don't we have to wait for the doctor to sign me out?"

She really was looking forward to leaving. The future may be uncertain, but she was ready to be moving forward and, more importantly, she wanted to see her daughter.

"He came in while you were in the bathroom." Dragon stepped up and gave her a kiss. "You do look beautiful."

"Thank you." Tari blushed. The relationship between them still felt rushed but she was doing her best to go with the flow. "So, we can *leave*?" The last word felt fuzzy and she wondered what language it had been.

"The nurse went to get a wheelchair. Tek is downstairs playing chauffeur." Dragon must have understood what she had asked.

She didn't want to admit that the idea of a wheelchair sounded amazing. She could walk, but every muscle ached, and she didn't know how far it was to the front doors. "Chauffeur?"

"I don't own a cage, so Tek offered to drive."

"Cage?" She worried that her brain had started hearing odd words.

Max laughed, relaxing her. "It's what bikers call cars. With that little girl you are going to have to buy a minivan, Dragon."

The look of horror on the sexy man's face was priceless. Tari wished she had a camera to capture the moment and decided to play along as she switched to Spanish. "*Oh, that would be amazing. With one of those video players in the ceiling, she could watch her princess movies when you are taking her to playdates.*"

Lali had never been on a playdate, and was much too young to start, but Dragon actually paled a bit and it was hard not to giggle.

"I... uh," Dragon sputtered.

She couldn't hold it in anymore and sat on the edge of the bed clutching her aching stomach as her giggles filled the room.

Max gave a small chuckle. "Good to know your woman has absolutely no poker face."

Dragon narrowed his eyes as if angry but the sparkle in

them told Tari he wasn't really mad. She was saved from whatever reprimand he would have delivered by the nurse coming in with the wheelchair.

The mood was light as they took her downstairs; Max and Dragon throwing friendly insults back and forth. A sleek, black Escalade was parked in front of the double doors with a handsome man leaning against the back door. If he hadn't been wearing a Dark Sons' cut Tari would have never guessed this clean-cut man was part of a motorcycle club.

The double doors opened as they got close and Dragon raised a hand in greeting. "Tek—"

Whatever else Dragon was going to say was cut off by the sound of glass shattering and loud bangs. Tari couldn't understand what was going on as she was knocked to the ground. Screams echoed around her as Dragon scooped her up in his arms. Max was shooting past the SUV at something she couldn't see. His left arm was dripping blood onto the ground. Over Dragon's shoulder she saw the nurse who had been pushing her being pulled backward by a security guard, blood staining the chest of her scrubs and painting the floor beneath her.

Automatic weapons exploded around them as Dragon practically dove with her through the now opened door of the SUV. Bullets pinged against the side of the vehicle somehow not shattering the glass. White starbursts in the glass kept her from being able to see the outside world. Tari twisted around trying to get her bearings, confused because the inside of the car reminded her more of a spaceship then anything she had ever seen. How were they going to survive this?

"Are you hit?" Dragon asked as he pulled up her shirt and scanned for new injuries.

Sitting on the floor, her back against one of the two plush seats, Tari took a minute to evaluate herself. Her stomach was sore as hell from the rough treatment, but nothing really hurt. "No."

The thuds of bullets hitting the car stopped and a minute later Tek was in the driver's seat and they were driving off at top speed.

"Max is going to see if he can catch the shooters on his bike," Tek said as he took a hard right out of the parking lot sending Dragon and her sliding on the floor. "I'm getting you and your woman back to the compound."

"Wasn't Max shot?" Tari was sure she had seen blood.

"Said it was just a graze," Tek responded coolly.

Tari maneuvered herself so she was sitting in one of the chairs and watched Dragon do the same. What kind of life did these men lead, that they could be shot and still get on a motorcycle to chase after someone? If shooting and high-speed chases were part of their everyday life, did she want her daughter being part of their world? A horrible thought crossed her mind and she launched herself at the man she was quickly falling in love with.

"*Oh my God, were you shot, Dragon?*" Tari started pawing at his clothes trying to see if he was bleeding anywhere.

"Your woman speaks Mandarin?" Tek asked as he took a turn and shot onto a highway without slowing.

"And nine other languages apparently." Dragon gripped her hands to stop her clumsy fumbling. "I'm fine, Tari. I wasn't hit."

He pulled her onto his lap, kissing the top of her head. Tari tried to relax and enjoy the sensation of being held as only he could. In his arms she felt small and feminine, but this time the adrenaline had everything racing in her body and she couldn't lose herself in the sensation.

"Call Deep," Tek's voice announced, followed by the sound of a phone ringing which cut off whatever she would have thought to say.

"You and your toys, Tek." Tari looked around at what had to be one of the most high-tech and luxurious cars she had ever seen. The back of the car was separated from the front with gadgets and computer screens on every surface that wasn't glass.

"Be glad I like my toys, or this Escalade wouldn't have an armor rating higher than most military vehicles."

A grumpy voice Tari didn't recognize filled the car. "It's Saturday morning and the kids are away, this better be important." Who was Deep and why was Tek calling him now?

Tek was polite enough not to voice his laugh. "Sorry, Brother, but you need to put your lawyer face on. We were just in the middle of a shootout at Denver Health. I've got Dragon and his woman in my car and we are fleeing the scene."

"Shit. You guys start it?"

Dragon spoke up, "No. If I had to guess it was a hit on my woman."

Tari wasn't sure if she liked, or hated, being claimed in such a caveman style. She tried to get up and move to her own seat but he held her still. His hands clenching down on her thighs had inappropriate thoughts flickering across her brain.

"Two guys in a POS car with automatic weapons opened up when Tari and Dragon started out the door," Tek added.

"Casualties?" Deep asked.

Dragon's voice rumbled in his chest as she settled against him deciding to take comfort in his arms. "Nurse hit but alive when we left and Max was grazed. Don't know if any other bystanders were hit, the idiots weren't being selective."

"Either of you pull weapons or fire?" Deep's voice was now all business.

"No, just Max," Tek answered.

"Okay, I'll deal with him later. What I'm hearing from you is a shooting broke out and, fearing for your life, you left. You have no other information that isn't pure speculation. I will contact the police and let them know you will be happy to answer any questions through me. Anything else?"

"None that can't wait." Dragon moved his hands slowly up and down her thigh. Tari was sure it was just a motion of comfort but the feel of his fingers brushing the soft cotton had her body coming alive for completely different reasons.

"Okay. You all heading to the compound?"

"Yes," Tek answered.

"Call me when you are there and I'll let you know what's next."

Tari shifted slightly and felt the evidence that Dragon was having the same inappropriate feelings she was. A part of her brain knew arousal was just the normal reaction to the adrenaline from being so close to death, but she couldn't get her body to relax. It needed an outlet. Her breathing became shallow as she imagined the perfect solution to both their problems.

They were alive and together. Her logical brain said now was not the time, but his hand was so high up on her thigh she couldn't stop her body from reacting to his touch. She looked up front to see Tek glancing in the rearview mirror.

"Will do." A beep sounded and she assumed the call was done.

She needed to get her hormones under control. While she admitted to enjoying watching others have sex on occasion, she never had the urge to be the show herself. Tari tried to stand again, figuring the only way to ease the situation was to put distance between her and Dragon.

The minute she had space between them, he had her by the hips and pulled her back down but now she was straddling his lap and their faces were inches apart. Unable to resist the temptation she fit her lips over his and kissed him. The warmth of his mouth was sweet for just a moment then he was claiming her.

Her sore stomach and tired muscles were barely a tiny thought as she was consumed by his kiss. Tari could feel the hard length of him contained in his jeans pressing against her core through the lightweight pants she wore.

How did this man short circuit every logical part of her brain with just a kiss? Dragon's hands slid under her shirt and cupped her breasts gently and she groaned wanting so much more but knowing they needed to stop.

"Dragon." His name was a plea but she didn't know if she was asking him to stop or keep going.

"I almost lost you again. I need you, *Mami*. I need to feel you alive, warm, and wrapped around my cock."

God, she needed that too, but a chuckle from the front helped her keep focused. "We can't do this right now. Later, *Papi*." A strange whirring sound came from behind her and she turned to see what made the noise. Her stomach spasmed as the movement pulled on the healing wounds and she winced in pain.

"I take it back, Tek, I love your toys," Dragon told Tek through a rising, black wall.

The black partition was rising and slowly shutting off the back from the front, like she had only seen in movies. Tari breathed through the pain, struggling with her body's conflicting needs. Now that they weren't going to have an audience she wanted to strip and climb on top of him, but she didn't think she could between muscle fatigue and the pain from her stomach.

"Are you okay?" Dragon's voice was soft with concern.

She cupped his cheek loving the way her dark skin looked against the warm amber of his. "I want you, Dragon. I want you so bad my panties are soaked but…"

"But what?"

Frustrated, she swept a hand down her stomach trying to find words that didn't make her feel weak. He smiled and brushed his thumb over her nipple sending a bolt of pleasure straight to her pussy.

"Don't worry, Tari. I'll be gentle but if I don't get to taste your sweet honey soon I'm going to go crazy. Kneel on the other chair and let me do all the work."

The deep sexy growl in his voice had her moving over. He moved the chair somehow and it started to recline. She was kneeling on the seat facing backward, almost hugging the headrest and her pulse raced as she wondered what he was going to do.

He pushed up her shirt and planted kisses slowly down her spine. Every brush of his lips was a pleasant little torture that slowly erased the aches of her injuries. By the time he pulled down her pants she was panting with need.

"I have dreamed about the taste of you for years. I can't wait to have your sweet pussy dripping on my tongue."

Dragon pushed her knees apart and his tongue swept up into her folds. The action was almost enough to trigger a small orgasm and she moaned her pleasure into the soft leather of the seat. He wasted no time, his fingers began circling her clit as he feasted at her entrance, licking, sucking, and nibbling; making her whole body ache with need.

She felt the orgasm building deep within her. She had missed this feeling so much. The knowledge that someone so special knew her body better than she did herself and used that to bring her to the highest heights. When his other hand started rimming her ass, she lost all control; the dirty pleasure too much to contain.

True to his word, she felt him sucking down her release, his tongue inside her while his fingers played with her clit dragging the orgasm out longer than she thought possible. He let her come down slowly. Tari moaned wanting more, needing him deep inside her. When she felt the length of him at her entrance she whimpered.

"Tell me what you want, *mi reina*." He slid his cock along her folds rubbing the head against her swollen clit.

"I need you, Dragon." Tari pushed back against him begging with her body for him to fill her.

He bit at her ear. "Give me the words. I want to hear that pretty mouth begging for dirty things." Dragon reached around, his hands finding and twisting her nipples in exquisite pleasure. "Can you be dirty for me, *Mami*? Just for me?"

His words tripped a switch inside her. "Please, *Papi*, fuck me. I want to feel your cock deep inside me."

In less than a second he slid home, deep and sudden. He was so big, for a moment it hurt, but then everything was right. She began orgasming with his first stroke. She forgot they were in a car, forgot what had happened earlier. Nothing mattered at that moment but the feel of him deep inside her; she screamed out her pleasure.

He began hammering her with sharp thrusts of his cock; rubbing wonderfully against her G-spot. Each push driving her to higher peaks with one orgasm folding into another.

"Your pussy is so fucking tight. *Cristo*, you're fucking perfect, you make me forget myself." Dragon started to pull out.

Confused, Tari looked back. "What's wrong?"

"Condom, *Mami*."

She bit her lip not sure if she should say anything but she loved the feel of him inside her bare. "I've gotten the shot since Lali was born." The cost had been hard to cover but even though she wasn't sleeping with anyone she hadn't wanted to risk an unplanned pregnancy again.

"Fuck. I'm clean I swear."

She nodded, and with a growl he was back inside her. His hands reached around her as his cock worked magic on her G-spot. He pinched her nipples as he thrust in and out of her quickly bringing her back to the edge of ecstasy.

Tari gasped as she reached another orgasm and the sensation continued to build. Lights began to dance in front of her eyes. The pleasure was too much and when she felt another orgasm building she wasn't sure she could survive it. Dragon's rhythm became jerky and she thought his orgasm would save her from her own.

"Dragon!" She felt him twist her nipples and the pleasure was too much. Fireworks shot off behind her eyes and she lost control of her body as the orgasm blinded her. This man was like a drug and she couldn't get enough. They panted together and her stomach twinged with a sharp pain.

Dragon was like a drug, but was that a good thing? This life, the danger, men who owned cars that could withstand bullets. Was this something that was good for her and her daughter?

Chapter 22

Yes we should forgive our enemies, but not until they are dead.

Dragon thought Tari's sleepy grumbles were the cutest thing he had ever heard. The sex had been amazing, but he had been concerned when she passed out at the end. She had woken up briefly when he cleaned her up, but she had almost immediately snuggled up in the chair and fallen back to sleep.

The doctor had warned she might sleep a lot at first and he hadn't probably intended for Tari to be so active. The gunfight had triggered every protective, possessive instinct he had. Even if he hadn't had the privacy of Tek's tricked out car, Dragon didn't think he could have waited.

Knowing his woman was still in danger tortured him. Thank all the saints she hadn't argued about going back to the compound. He knew his Brothers would keep her safe and help him eliminate whoever it was trying to harm her. Joining the Dark Sons had been the best decision he had ever made.

Civilians couldn't understand the Brotherhood that these men represented. He had felt that loyalty and certainty of purpose when he was in the SEALs and finding it outside the military was priceless.

The divider slowly lowered and Tek looked back and chuckled at the sleeping woman in the back seat.

"We're almost there. Sounded like you guys were done so I thought I'd let you know."

"Sounded?"

Tek grinned into the rearview. "My ride may be bullet-proof, but it's not soundproofed."

Dragon shrugged not caring much. "Glad you picked this ride to take us home. Don't think things would have worked out as well if we had taken Puck's truck."

Dragon had planned to ask his newest Brother to drive them but, after the party for getting patched in, Puck was still hungover two days later.

"Lady Luck must like you because I usually only use this on ops for the company or if I need a mobile office. I don't usually drive it. I will be giving Mitch a bonus for convincing me to put out the extra cash for the armor."

Dragon knew Mitch was the head of the mercenary arm of Tek's company. He wasn't a Brother, but he would some-times come and hang out with them. "How much did this ride cost?"

"This upgraded model costs over $75,000."

"Damn. Glad you have that kind of cash to spare."

Tek shrugged. Dragon respected his Brother even more. Even after making billions, and being CEO of a major secu-rity corporation, he would do shit like volunteer to pick up a Brother and his woman at the hospital. Tek never shirked doing anything for the Dark Sons and gave the MC digital security that was unrivaled in the US.

"Max called while you were busy."

"Did he catch the shooters?" Dragon hoped if he had that the Brother saved a piece of them for him.

"No, by the time he tried to follow they were gone, but he said he recognized the driver."

"Who was it?" If they knew who it was, Dragon would get Tari settled in at the compound then ride out and end this shit.

"Chobo."

"I thought we hadn't gotten the info on that name yet." Dragon was pissed. They had started the search for an identity for that asshole yesterday after Tari's nightmare, but as far as he knew they had drawn a blank.

"I'm guessing you haven't checked your email this morning. I found a picture and some details, but don't have a location on him yet."

Dragon hadn't even looked at his email in the last two days. Someone should have called or texted him. "What do we know?"

"Mid-level player in the Jacks. Other than one arrest for assault, we don't have much. He doesn't have a known address or workplace."

The Jacks kept showing up wherever he looked. "You think this was random or has to do with Dark Zen."

Tek chuckled and Dragon saw they were pulling into the compound. "Still can't believe the Club owns a place with the word Zen in it. I don't know. Her first attack could have been random, but then why go after her again when they know that is going to bring us down on their heads?"

"Guess we'll have to just ask them when we find them."

Chapter 23

I'm usually sweet, but if you make me mad, remember I always have a pocketful of crazy waiting to come out!

Tari slowly woke, an unfamiliar fuzzy pillow was under her cheek. Wherever she was smelled of lemon cleaner covering a faint scent of smoke and stale beer. The room was quiet except for the sound of two women whispering nearby. It took a minute for her to understand the words and fear evident in their quiet tones.

"They are so big, Yana. Will they hurt us?"

"I don't know, Daria."

They were speaking Ukrainian with what Tari thought was a western accent probably coming from somewhere near Poland. Why was she laying down on what felt like a couch in a room with women she didn't recognize? The last thing she remembered was being with Dragon in the back of the car. A flush crept up her cheeks as she remembered what they had been doing.

Tari opened her eyes, but the visual of her surroundings didn't help much. She was in a large room with almost a bar or club feel. She was, in fact, on an old couch with a blanket over her and a folded fleece blanket under her cheek as a pillow. Two women sat huddled on a couch that was next to her own. Though calling them women might be stretching the truth, girls was more accurate.

They looked similar enough, with ash blonde hair and green eyes, they were probably sisters. The older, who might possibly be eighteen but was probably only sixteen or seventeen, held the younger in a protective hug. Tari would have bet all her savings that the younger girl wasn't a day over fourteen.

"I can't do a group of big men again. Please tell them I'll do anything, just not that." Bile rose in Tari's throat as she realized what the younger girl, Daria, thought was going to happen.

Yana looked around the room as if looking for an escape, while she rubbed circles on Daria's back. *"None of them have looked at you with hunger. Maybe they will leave you be and only want me and this other woman they knocked out."*

Tari sat up, taking stock of herself. Had something bad happened while she slept? She was sore all over but was sure she had just been asleep, not knocked out. Could she have slept through being kidnapped? She didn't think so.

"Maybe she knows what they want, ask her."

Yana gave Tari a hesitant look making her feel sorrow for the two terrified girls. "Know why we is here?" The girl's English was so heavily accented that it was painfully obvious she barely spoke English.

Tari looked around trying to make sense of the situation. Across the room she saw three rough looking men all wearing the black leather vests she recognized as Dark Sons' cuts. My God did the Dark Sons have a hot men only policy? It was really kind of ridiculous that every one of them was in what looked like peak physical condition. Only one looked familiar and she racked her brain for his name. Did Dragon's Club kidnap girls? She wanted to reassure the girls they were safe but she wasn't sure.

Deciding to find out what she could, she asked the girls in Ukrainian, *"How did you end up here?"*

Both girls looked relieved when she spoke their language. *"Big men broke into the place Master V keeps us and started asking questions. But they were angry we couldn't understand them. They dragged us back here and another man tried talking to us in Russian but we don't speak that. Then they brought you in and most of them went back there."* Daria's words were said in a rushed whisper as if she feared being overheard.

"Master V?"

"He is our owner. Do you think that he sold us or did they steal us?" Yana didn't seem to know which option was scarier.

Bile rose in Tari's throat. That the girl spoke of being owned like it was normal sent shivers down her spine. Slavery was something the ignorant and privileged couldn't believe existed in the US but right here was proof they were wrong. Young girls trapped in what had to be hell was more than Tari could stomach.

Daria's earlier words echoed in her mind '*I can't do a group of big men again*'. The thought of what these two girls had obviously already survived had Tari fighting back vomit. She might believe there were motorcycle clubs that sunk to that low, but she could not believe for one moment that Dragon would be part of any group that would buy and sell underage girls.

"Flak." Tari called out to the only man she recognized. She had only met the tall dark-haired Italian man once, but she was sure he would either tell her what was going on or get Dragon for her. The girls on the couch next to her huddled in on themselves. The looks on their faces clearly stating they thought her insane to draw attention to herself. "*I will find out what is going on,"* Tari murmured trying to show with her calm there was nothing to fear.

Flak turned his head, a smile lighting up his handsome face when he saw she was the one calling to him. He said something to the men next to him, then strode over. "Sleeping beauty wakes. What can I do for you?"

Tari was surprised by how casual and welcoming the big bad biker was. She had only met him briefly when he took over a shift on guard duty, but he acted as if they were long-time friends. That had to be a good sign, right?

She tried to echo his attitude while showing the girls there was nothing to fear. "Where's Dragon?" She thought she was more likely to get answers from Dragon.

"They're in Church. He told me to get you whatever you needed until they're done."

Tari had a vague memory of her roommate telling her that Church is what these men called their Club meetings. Pain spiked in her head as she tried to remember more but it slipped away. She felt the fuzziness she had learned meant her mind was not quite right. She took several breaths to focus so her words would come out in English. "How long will they be in there?"

"Till they're done." Flak smirked and Tari barely resisted the urge to growl.

Where was her calm? The last few days had eroded the peace she was normally able to wrap around herself. "Fine. Can you tell me why these girls are here?"

"That's Club business, sweet stuff. Can I get you a drink or something to eat?" Flak's tone held ice that Tari didn't like one bit.

"It's Club business to kidnap underage Ukrainian girls? What? Can't find enough local sluts to sleep with? *Tu madre debe estar muy orgullosa.*" Tari felt her control slipping and didn't care what language she was now shouting. "*I'll cut your balls off and feed them to you! If you think I'm just going to sit here and let you do what want—"*

"Relax, Tari." Flak held his hands up as if trying to placate her but the rage inside her was like an out-of-control inferno. She took a deep breath to tell him where he could shove his platitude when blinding daggers of pain racked her brain and her mind dragged her into a memory.

"Ahhh!" Her voice cracked as she gripped her head feeling as if it would break apart. Like a movie on fast forward the night she had been attacked played through her thoughts. The pain, fear, and desperation just as sharp as if it was all happening again. Every moment crystal clear and she screamed as she felt the knife slicing into her again. Then it started again and again.

Strong hands grabbed her and she lashed out throwing whatever came to hand, wanting to fight like she hadn't been able to that night. She kicked, cursed, and thrashed trying to kill the men all around her.

"You won't hurt my baby!"

"*Cristo,* stop fighting me, Tari. Calm down no one is going to hurt our daughter she is with Mama."

Dragon's voice finally cut through the replaying nightmare and she felt all her strength pour out of her along with the red haze of her rage. His grip eased as he pulled her against his chest, stroking her hair. She looked around and found the room was now filled with about twenty men. Their expressions all a varied mix of amusement, confusion, and pity.

Yana and Daria were curled into the corner of the couch trying to make themselves as small as possible. She recognized some of the men from her time in the hospital, but others were strangers. How many men belonged to the Dark Sons? Every one of them looked lethal, even the few older men who looked to be in their fifties.

"What happened, *mi reina?*" Dragon's deep voice was so

soothing she felt her calm starting to return as she breathed in his intoxicating male scent.

"It was a flashback *to that* night." She now remembered every moment of that nightmare, but she didn't let herself slide back there. She concentrated on her breath, her heartbeat searching for the centered place that allowed her to find clarity in the most difficult of times.

"What set you off? Was it a dream?" He kept stroking her hair and she wished they were alone so she wouldn't have to talk in front of these virtual strangers.

Tari looked up into Dragon's dark eyes and sent a silent prayer out that what she feared couldn't be real. Switching to Spanish and lowering her voice she hoped only he would hear her next question but with so many of them close it was unlikely to be private. *"Does your Club deal in trafficking sex slaves?"* She swallowed and looked over at the girls forcing the next words out on a shaky breath. *"Of underage girls?"*

The look of horror and disgust filling his face soothed something inside her as he pulled back. The anger and hurt in his eyes that followed made her wince. *"You think I'd—"*

"Okay. Show's over." A large man bellowed. Power seemed to just exude from him reminding Tari of the embodiment of a God of war. His voice held a hint of NY and his dark brown hair was laced with gray. On the right side of his cut were patches that read Hawk and President. The way all the men quickly backed off left no doubt in Tari's mind that he was the man in charge. "Officers in my office. Dragon, bring your woman. Max, bring the girls. We are sorting this shit out now."

Chapter 24

Assumptions are the termites of relationships. – Henry Winkler

D ragon tried to hide his unease as he settled Tari into a chair. He rarely ever came into Hawk's inner sanctum and didn't like that he had to bring his woman there to face some of the scariest Brothers in the Club. Hawk, Dozer, Sharp, Highdive, Tek, and Max were enough to frighten the best special ops team. The room was done up in dark woods and the walls and shelves covered with pictures of Brothers and military memorabilia. Several chairs were in the office and it felt crowded with seven large men and three women.

He wanted to be alone with Tari, figuring out why she thought such horrible things about his Club. But he knew Hawk had overheard her words and understood them. A private talk was no longer an option. The Brothers had just been discussing what to do about their suspicions of a sex ring, and what to do with the girls, when Tari's screams and curses had echoed through the Clubhouse drawing Church to an abrupt end.

The sight of her hurling insults and furniture at Flak was something he wouldn't soon forget. The realization that she was in a full-blown waking flashback had gutted him. The strong vibrant woman who had filled his dreams for two years was now shadowed with darkness.

It was his fault. He hadn't been there to protect her or their child. She had struggled alone and been victim to brutal assholes who had hurt her so badly she experienced waking nightmares. Even now that they were reunited, he had obviously failed her if she believed he and his Brothers would sell young girls for sex. He had a long way to go to earn her trust and respect if she believed for even one moment that something like that was true.

Hawk cleared his throat. "Since Church was interrupted, so we could save our prospect from getting abused by Dragon's woman, I figure we can have this discussion with a smaller audience." Dragon tried not to smirk as Tari's eyes dropped to her hands and the cutest expression of embarrassment filled her face. "Max, what did you find out from the girls?"

"Nothing really. Their language is Slavic, but I only speak Russian and a touch of Czech."

"It's Ukrainian," Tari mumbled into her chest, her nostrils flaring in that cute way they did when she was breathing deep trying to be calm.

Hawk raised an eyebrow. "I'm assuming you know that because you speak it?" She nodded. "And that would be why you accused us of human trafficking and selling underage girls for sex."

Sharp cursed and rage filled his features. "You think that? You're friends with two of this Club's Old Ladies, you're sleeping with one of my Brothers. Brothers who have saved your life twice and guarded your ass day and night. You think we're scum like that!"

Dragon stepped between Sharp and Tari. He knew his Brother was especially sensitive on this topic since Pixie, his Old Lady, had been saved from human trafficking just a few months ago. Dragon might not know what was going on in his woman's mind, but he wouldn't let Sharp vent that rage in her direction.

Tari not knowing when to shut up waved at the two girls now huddled in a corner near Highdive. "You're holding them hostage. And I woke up to hear a girl barely starting puberty begging her sister to convince you all to only take her one at a time because she couldn't handle a gangbang... *again.*"

Growls of masculine anger filled the room; only quieting when the whimpers of fear from the girls registered. Highdive, who never showed anything coming close to a soft side, cursed and stepped away from the girls, trying unsuccessfully to look less intimidating.

Dragon stared at the woman who had filled every moment of his thoughts for the last week. "You really think that of me and my Brothers?" He wasn't proud of just how hurt his tone was.

"No. Not really. I don't know. Why are you holding them against their will?" Tari's voice shook and it broke his heart.

"Because we went to check out the address listed on most of Dark Zen's mystery employees." Sharp ran a frustrated hand through his hair. "We found them naked and locked in a room in the basement. What were we supposed to do? Just leave them there?"

Dragon knew Sharp was leaving out a lot for Tari's sake. He had described the encounter in detail during Church earlier. Before his Brothers had managed to break down the door and kill the two fuckers who had been guarding the shit-hole house, the thugs had managed to kill four other girls.

These two had been the only survivors. The identification on the men had led to no gang or affiliation yet. But the two did have records with a list of crimes that should have had the men still rotting in jail; not out abusing more women.

"I don't know. What are you going to do with them then?" His woman sounded contrite, but it still bothered Dragon that she could think such horrible things about him and his Brothers.

"We need to know what they know," Hawk said his tone gentle. "Normally, I wouldn't let a Civilian get involved in Club business. But since you speak their language, why don't you help us out? Once we know what they know, we'll figure something out that will keep them safe until they can make it on their own."

It hurt to hear Hawk calling his woman a Civilian, as if she wasn't part of the Dark Sons' Club, but officially she was still that. His Brothers would protect her for him because she was the mother of his kid, but until he made her his Old Lady, she wasn't family. Truthfully, even if she were his Old Lady, she would be kept outside the loop on most things for her own safety. The fact that the Club was going to help these girls was, yet another reason Dragon was proud to be a Dark Son. His Brothers may not care much about laws, but they did what they saw as right and protected their own.

Tari nodded her agreement. She sat down on the couch with the girls and took their hands in her own. He loved the gentle tone she used with them even if he couldn't understand the words. Slowly over time they relaxed and started talking with Tari.

Dragon was proud of how calm she was. She pulled the younger of the two girls into her lap and looked up. "She says they've been in the US for a few months. A man named Master V was in charge. They were forced to service multiple men a day, sometimes in groups. If they resisted, they were beaten and starved."

Dragon tried to match his Tari's calm so as not to scare the girls but it was hard. Tek handed her a box of tissues and she wiped the girls' eyes and her own. His woman was magnificent: giving comfort and coaxing in equal measure.

She got names, descriptions, and places they had been and what had happened to them. It slowly formed a picture that had every man in the room ready to destroy any person who had a part in hurting the two girls, only fourteen and seventeen, who had come legally to this country to find a better life.

When the women were emotionally spent, and no one thought they could get any more information out of them, Dragon set the three up in the kitchen. Pixie cooked a large, late lunch for the four of them, before he returned to Hawk's office to find out what the Dark Sons were going to do about the evil they had just discovered in their own backyard.

Chapter 25

We're going to be kicking ass and taking names... actually no need for names.

"**F**UCK!" Dragon heard Sharp's yell as he opened the door. Now that the women were gone the men weren't holding back their fury. Sharp and Highdive looked like they were about to run out and beat someone to death with their fists. Muscles clenched and hot fury in their eyes.

Tek paced with his phone against his head. "I want the entire cyber investigation team researching those coordinates. No, they can wait. I don't care. Steal a fucking satellite feed if you have to, but get it done!" His words and tone clipped as if each word was a struggle to get out.

It was Hawk and Max's reaction that had Dragon pausing in his own fury a second before closing the door, not sure if he was still wanted among the Officers. Both men were so cold you could almost feel it emanating from them. It was the look of someone who was about to burn the city to the ground and smile at the flames. All the Dark Sons were dangerous, most with military backgrounds kept current with training, so much so, that even an ex-SEAL like Dragon, considered it impressive. He had no doubt the five men in this room had the skills and resources to take over a small nation if they ever wanted.

"How did we miss this?" Hawk's question brought all attention to him. Tek hung up his call and they all came to stand in front of the desk like they were back in the military about to get ripped apart by a commanding officer.

Max spoke first. "It was a girlie spa Dozer wanted to buy to make his Old Lady happy. None of us thought it was a high-risk investment, so we didn't look below the surface. We fucked up."

"Hell, when Sharp and I went over to that address today, worst I thought we would find was some women who gave the customers a little extra for cash," Highdive said.

"We only busted into the place because the fuckers slammed the door in our faces, and we heard a woman's scream," Sharp added.

"Do we have any idea who this 'Master V' is?" Hawk looked at each one of them in turn.

"Overweight, middle-aged, white man. Could be half the city. I'll need to find a sketch artist I trust to keep their mouth shut, since, I'm assuming, we won't be going to the cops with this." Tek's tone said he didn't have issue with that fact.

Dragon didn't either. The justice system was fucked up and sitting in a cushy jail, or getting off on a technicality, wasn't going to cut it this time. Men were buying and abusing young girls and they had used a Dark Sons' business to do it.

"Sit down, let's talk this through." Hawk gestured to the many chairs in the room and moved out from behind his desk to take the closest as if trying to put everyone on equal ground. Everyone sat, but none of them were relaxed. Dragon wasn't used to being part of these types of discussions with the Officers and appreciated they included him because of Tari's connection.

"Something isn't right with this situation. If the girls were a Jacks operation, why weren't some of their members guarding the place?" Max said.

"Jacks have maybe 25 men in their crew, 30 if we account for members the cops don't know about. Most of them are teens." Tek shook his head. "They have no national organization and the only reason they have power is the heroin they deal and the guns they own. They have minor ties to the cartel through their leader Diablo. If they were running girls, I would think Mexican not Eastern European."

Dragon agreed a lot of things weren't making sense. If the Jacks had been into human trafficking for long, something would have popped up months ago when they were dealing with Pixie's problems. He had an idea. "What if Chobo and that other guy—"

"Tico," Tek supplied.

"Right, Tico, were just side players letting this V guy use Dark Zen as a front in return for cash or other considerations?"

"You're thinking the drugs and the women were separate?" Hawk scratched his jaw considering.

"You think Diablo knows his boys were running a side business?" Highdive asked.

Hawk seemed to consider for a minute then nodded. "My meeting with Diablo is tonight. If he doesn't show, we'll know he was in on the attack at the hospital. Fucker has brass balls, but I doubt he would be dumb enough to face us if he ordered his men to pull that stunt. Tek, pull everything we have on the two we know are involved. Sharp, I want you and two other snipers in position tonight just in case. Dragon, Max, and Highdive you'll be with me. We go in suited up and ready. One way or another I'm getting answers tonight, even if we have to gut every one of those punks to do it."

Chapter 26

Don't go to bed angry. Stay up and fight.

"Mama mama mama."

Tari couldn't hide her joy when she turned from the table to see her wriggling daughter reaching out to her, while being carried in by Dragon's mother. She stood up, reaching her arms out for her beautiful little girl. The weight, when Lali threw herself into her arms, was unexpectedly hard to hold and Tari stumbled a step before she caught herself.

"Careful, *mija*. The doctors told you not to strain yourself." Mama Rios calling her daughter touched a soft spot in Tari's heart. Her adoptive mom had never referred to her by anything but her full name, to have this woman she only just met offer such affection was almost overwhelming.

"I'll be okay, Mama Rios." Tari snuggled Lali a bit closer taking in her clean, wonderful smell. She had almost lost her daughter; the rekindled memories all too fresh in her mind. "Have you been having fun, sweetie?"

Light danced in the little girl's eyes and Tari was so glad her daughter was too young to understand or remember the horrible things surrounding both of them. "Aba cookies yeah!" She squealed.

Mama Rios chuckled. "*Abuela.*"

Lali scrunched up her face. "*Abeyha.*"

Tari laughed. "You'll have *her speaking Spanish in no time.*"

"Talk funny, Mama!" Lali's confused expression just about broke her heart.

Mama Rios smiled. "Spanish is not funny, *Princesa*, its beautiful."

"Bootiful!" Lali giggled.

Tari felt like a failure. The day had been like a roller-coaster and she was already exhausted. Her arms were starting to shake a bit from the strain of lifting her little girl.

Pixie saved her from having to put her down by holding out her arms. "Who wants some fruit?"

Lali launched herself and the tiny woman caught her with an expert's touch as she settled Lali onto her hip. Tari admired how Pixie so effortlessly helped and supported everyone around her, even though her own baby bump was becoming bigger by the day.

"Lope!" Her daughter's vocabulary was still limited so each word was a surprise to Tari. With the gaps in her memory she didn't even remember what Lali's first word was or at what point she had become such a chatterbox. Would she ever get her memory and strength back?

Exhaustion pulled at her and tears pricked her eyes. Her only contribution to these people who had stepped in and saved her daughter and herself had been as translator which probably could have been handled just as well by an app on the phone. How could she even start to repay them?

She hadn't even been able to get the two girls settled. The apartment on the compound they had been given was just too far of a walk and Val had taken the scared girls. Tari's rational mind knew the doctor had said it would take time for her mind and body to heal, but she wasn't feeling particularly rational.

Tari was drawn from her spiraling thoughts as Sharp and Dragon entered the kitchen. Lali was sitting in a highchair with melon pieces all cut up in front of her. Dragon bent down for a kiss and instead received a raised offering of cantaloupe.

"I think that is for you, little girl." Dragon chuckled.

"Papa, lope!" Lali pressed the soggy fruit against her father's lips.

He made wide eyes then opened his mouth wide and bit down. "Nam Nam Nam." Tari held back a laugh and Dragon continued play nibbling up Lali's arm ending with a smacking kiss on her cheek which sent their little girl into peals of laughter.

"There is no sound in this world more precious than that of a child's laugh," Mama Rios whispered beside her.

Tari nodded her agreement, unable to talk past the lump of emotion in her throat. Dragon picked his daughter up and carried her over. He leaned down and brushed a kiss against her mouth.

Tari couldn't help but lick her lips, the sweet flavor making her smile. "Cantaloupe kisses mmm."

Heat flared in Dragon's eyes and, for a moment, she felt like the two of them were alone in the world sharing an attraction that was indescribable. How strong was their connection, that just a brief chaste kiss could scramble her thoughts and make her forget everything but him? He cupped her face gently.

"You look tired, *mi reina*."

Tari cut off her yawn trying to pretend she didn't want to curl up and sleep. "I'm fine."

Dragon's lips thinned, and his tone went harsh. "Don't lie to me."

"Gabor give your woman a break. You men think you are strong but until you birth a baby you know nothing of what strength is," Mama Rios chided her son in Spanish.

It was strange, but nice, to have someone stand up for her. Dragon winced at his mother's words and Tari found herself hiding a grin.

"Sorry, Mama."

"Is the little princess ready for her sleepover with Aunty Pixie and Aunty Val?" Pixie skipped over smiling.

"What? No, you don't have to do that. *Nosotras estaremos bien.*" Tari was confused. While the idea of having to take care of Lali with her current level of exhaustion was daunting, she couldn't keep imposing on them.

"You are still recovering." Pixie waved off her concerns. "And there is no way I'm going to call Val and tell her that playtime and cuddle time is cancelled."

Sharp came up behind his woman and cradled her stomach in his big hands. He kissed the side of her neck. "You won't be fine, Tari if you don't rest. You can pay us back when our little girl is here so we can get some alone time."

When put like that it was hard to refuse. This Club and its sense of community seemed like what she should have had within her own commune. How was it that a bunch of outlaw bikers understood more of what family was supposed to be, than a group of supposed righteous missionaries? If it wasn't for the danger and violence that surrounded these men, Tari could easily see herself loving being part of them.

"Okay, if you're sure."

"Absolutely." Pixie smiled reaching for Lali who eagerly went to her.

It hurt just a little that her daughter so willingly went to a woman who wasn't her. Tari leaned in and kissed Lali's cheek. "I love you, baby."

When Lali was out the door, Tari squeaked as Dragon scooped her up in his arms. She should probably protest but she was too tired to do so. Being carried around like she weighed nothing was oddly comforting to Tari. At 5'11" she never thought she would find a man who treated her like she was small and delicate but, against Dragon's 6'6" extremely muscled frame, that was exactly what she was. But things felt strained between them. The connection was still there but, ever since she accused his Club earlier, it was like there was an invisible wall muting it. He was taking her upstairs to a room where she could rest, and she hoped they could talk things out.

The upstairs of the Dark Sons' Clubhouse looked more like a hotel than anything else. Closed doors lined the hallways, some painted red, but most primer white with a few glossy black ones thrown in for good measure. Dragon stopped in front of a white door and maneuvered them inside. The room reminded her of a slightly smaller version of what she had been renting for the last year. A king-sized bed took up most of the room but there was a small desk and dresser.

Dragon laid her gently down on the bed. The silence between them was killing her so she blurted out the first thing that came to mind. "What is with the different color doors?"

Dragon's lip lifted in a knowing smirk. "Black doors are the Officers reserved rooms. White are for when Brothers crash here."

"And the red?"

"Party rooms." Mischief sparkled in Dragon's eyes.

"Party. Why don't I think that means you have cake and appetizers in there?"

"That is where Brothers go to fuck when they welcome company. If they close the door it means they're with a woman and want privacy, but don't plan on spending the night with them."

"Oh." Interesting images of people doing things she only had ever read about flashed in her mind and had her heart speeding up. "Do you use those rooms often?"

Dragon took a gentle yet firm grip on her chin and forced her to look him in the eyes. "If you're asking if I fucked around with women, I'm not going to lie to you, yes, but there was never anyone special. If you're asking if I want to take you into those rooms listen closely, *Mami*. I will not share you. I will fulfil every dirty fantasy you have as long as it doesn't involve another man laying one finger on you."

Tari's thighs clenched as desire flowed through her. She had never fantasized about two men fucking her so it wouldn't be an issue. The idea of watching two or more men fuck another woman, that was a different story. She had always been that way, watching and listening to people fascinated her, and when those people were having sex, well that got her fired up faster than oil near a flame.

"I don't want anyone else touching me either."

"Good."

"Or other women touching you."

"Of course."

Tari swore she could almost hear his thoughts as they played behind his eyes. She definitely felt the emotional distance growing between them as he stood and walked over to the dresser. The effort of maintaining English was too much so she switched to Spanish.

"Talk to me, Dragon. I'm sorry about what I said earlier, please don't pull away."

He pulled out a large shirt from the drawer and handed it to her. "You need sleep and I've got a run tonight with the Brothers."

"You're leaving?" Fear rushed through her veins like ice

water. She didn't know if it was fear of him leaving or fear of being alone.

"I've got Club business tonight. You'll be safe here with my Brothers and we'll talk in the morning."

"*You have to go right now?*"

"No, but you need your sleep. You can use that to sleep in." Dragon lifted his chin to indicate the shirt she was now clutching.

"*If you think I can sleep knowing you're still mad at me, you're crazy.*" Tari was exhausted but knew she would toss and turn trying to think of ways to fix things. She didn't know exactly what this thing between them was going to become but she did know she wanted to try and make it work.

"I'm not mad, Tari. I'm…" He ran a hand down the side of his face sighing. "I'm just disappointed."

Strangely, that hurt Tari more than if he had been angry. She had heard many times from her parents how she constantly disappointed them. "Because of what I asked?"

"Because you could believe for even one second that I, that my Brothers could be part of something like that. I know you haven't known the Club or, hell, even me long; but have you ever seen anything from one of us that would make you think we are the kind of evil that could do that?"

"*No. But Dragon you have to understand I don't know anything about motorcycle clubs that I haven't learned from gossip, TV, or romance novels. And they all say that 'yeah you protect your own but if someone isn't part of the club they don't matter'.*"

Dragon raised an eyebrow. "You read MC romance books?"

Of course that would be what he focused on. "*That is not the point.*"

He chuckled and the sound had something relaxing deep inside her. "You're right, it's not." Dragon sighed and came over sitting next to her on the bed then put his arm around her. The warmth and comfort of his body so close had her laying her head into the crook of his shoulder. "I forgot that even if you had every one of your memories back, we haven't had time to really get to know each other. It just feels like we've known each other forever."

"*I feel that too, but then things happen, and I realize how little I really know.*" Tari wanted to know everything about Dragon. Her heart believed she could trust this man who had so quickly claimed a part of her soul. But she wasn't a young single girl who could just take a leap of faith. She was a mother. Keeping her daughter safe and providing a stable, healthy environment trumped her heart's desires.

"What do you want to know?" He kissed her on the top of her head.

Tari wasn't sure where to begin. The two of them had been thrown into this whirlwind that sped every decision up. Instead of having months or years to learn each other and grow closer, they had a daughter who tied them together forever and they needed to find stable ground. Sexual compatibility wouldn't be enough, though they had plenty of that. Tari decided to start with the one part of his life that might be a line in the sand.

"*Why did you join a Motorcycle Club?*"

She felt his chest rise and fall a few times before he answered and was glad he wasn't just blurting something out.

"Brotherhood. When I joined the SEALs, I found something I had been missing. A purpose that was bigger than just me. More than the missions and men who had my back, I had a purpose. No matter where I was or what I was doing I trusted the men around me to put us and the mission above anything else."

Tari could see why that feeling would appeal. She had always longed to be part of a community that cherished its members rather than expecting the members to serve blindly.

"I met Sharp on my first tour. He was a member of the Dark Sons in Texas back then, but Hawk was talking to him about starting a chapter in Colorado; so, he asked me about my home state. When we got leave, he visited and met my family."

"*So, you joined because of Sharp?*" Tari was amazed that a friendship could be so strong you shaped your life around it.

"More than that. Sharp left the service the next year and we didn't really keep in contact. I had a drink with him once or twice when I was on leave since he started the chapter in Denver. But four years ago my sister Kachina was in trouble. Her husband had started drinking and using his fists on her and the kids. She left him and moved in with Mama, but he wasn't stopping his abuse."

"*I'm so sorry, that is awful.*"

"I had months before my next leave, and the cops and the restraining orders weren't helping. I was desperate, so I called Sharp."

"*He helped her out?*"

"The whole Club did. Gave them a safe place, managed to get the bastard to sign over parental rights, and move to the East Coast. But they also helped my sister until she got back on her feet. I wasn't a Brother yet, but because I was friends with Sharp and on active duty, they made sure my family was safe."

Tari couldn't imagine how much that must have meant to a man who must have felt powerless over an ocean away. Men, in her experience, hated asking for help and that must have been doubly hard for someone like him who was trained by the military to handle all situations.

"I asked to become a prospect on my next leave but Sharp wouldn't let me. He said joining because of gratitude wasn't the right reason. I needed to get to know the Brothers first. It took two years before he said yes, and I don't regret it for one second."

His story was amazing, but Tari wasn't a young naive girl. Getting rid of an abusive man probably hadn't been accomplished with stern words or actions that were completely legal. The question that really bothered her was, where was the line drawn and could she live with it? Even more concerning, could she raise a daughter knowing she would be exposed to it.

Caught up in her own thoughts Tari didn't realize she had been rubbing her hand up and down Dragon's chest until he stopped her hand with his own and kissed her again on top of the head.

"We aren't choir boys, Tari and, by the letter of the law, every one of us has done things that could mean time in jail. But we do it for reasons and people we believe in."

She wasn't surprised Dragon knew where her real worries started. The two of them had a connection she didn't understand. She wished she could just let go and follow her heart but it wasn't that easy. "*It is just hard when I don't get to know the whole picture. In just the last few hours, it has become clear you won't ever be able to share everything with me. 'Club business' is a phrase I think I might come to hate.*"

"Military wives have the same problems and, unfortunately, it isn't something I can say will change without lying to you."

"*Do you have to go away for long periods of time too?*" Tari was teasing him, but his comparison was making sense of a situation she was struggling with.

"Not nearly as long as a deployment lasts; but sometimes yeah, we go on jobs that take us away from home for a few weeks."

"*Oh. And you'll never be able to talk about the Club?*"

"Not everything is a secret. If I don't share something it

will either be to protect you or someone else. I can promise not to lie but, you need to understand, when I say I can't share, it isn't personal."

That thought was hard to swallow but it was something Tari guessed was a struggle for more than just people associated with motorcycle clubs. The question was, did she trust Dragon and his Brothers?

"I want Lali to have a normal life."

"Ah *querida*." Dragon tilted her face up so they were looking into each other's eyes. "What is normal? She will be surrounded by an extended family who will fill her life with love. She will have so many protective uncles she will probably grow to hate it as she gets older. But you will know no matter what happens, my Brothers will be there for you and her."

Tari didn't want to think of a future without Dragon. All her doubts and questions didn't change the growing love in her heart for this man. She could see the same wealth of emotion reflected back at her in his eyes.

"That sounds like you think something is going to happen to you."

"No, *Mami*. If it is up to me, we will grow old in each other's arms. But it is smart to have plans."

Tari couldn't resist the draw of his lips anymore. She leaned in and kissed him with all the emotion bubbling inside of her. They kissed gently, both knowing the conversation wasn't over but wanting to show each other how they felt. There were so many things they still had to worry about and figure out, but for once Tari had real hope. Her heart was telling her she loved this man and everything else would work itself out.

Chapter 27

A wise man once said, "Don't start a fight with a man who can end you from another zip code."

'*Tek always gives us the best toys'* Grinder's voice came over Dragon's bone conduction earpiece. Despite the noise of his motorcycle the sound quality was amazing.

'*I thought your M82 was the best toy?*' Sharp said.

'*Ah but she isn't a toy. She is a work of art.*'

'*Are you gentlemen going to give me a sitrep or just jerk off about your equipment?*' Hawk's voice cut through the banter.

Sharp, Grinder, and Rooster had gone ahead to the meet site hours earlier to set themselves up in Sniper positions. Dragon rode alongside Max, Highdive, and Hawk fully decked out for the first time in state-of-the-art combat armor under black BDUs. The bullet proof material wasn't comfortable while riding but they all believed it might be needed. They were driving public streets so they couldn't carry all the hardware Dragon would have liked, but they did have several handguns visible as well as heavier backup weapons in their saddlebags.

'*Looks like Diablo brought twenty men with him including our pal, Tico,*' Sharp reported.

'*How long have they been there?*' Highdive asked.

'*Pulled up about fifteen minutes ago in five cars. They have a hooded hostage bound in the back of the car parked furthest away. Two tough guys are holding automatic rifles like they learned how to shoot from a bad gangster movie. Everyone else has the standard gangbanger piece down their pants pointed at their prides and joy.*'

'*It's like they want us to make fun of them.*' Max chuckled.

'*We're two minutes out. Do you all have full coverage?*' Hawk asked.

Grinder chuckled. '*We have 360 coverage and, at this distance with what I'm packing, even hiding behind the car would be pointless. If you request a maiming, the pansy crap Sharp or Rooster are holding have less chance of removing the limb.*"

'*Good. Let's get our game faces on. One way or another, we are settling this shit.*'

Diablo, the Jacks' leader, had picked the meeting spot: the middle of a parking lot in an abandoned shopping center. He probably thought the open terrain meant no surprises. Unfortunately for him, Dark Sons had plenty of Brothers who could make a kill shot from a mile away. The three men here wouldn't find the less than 200 meters from the surrounding rooftops a challenge.

Dragon easily found the cold place inside him where he went while on missions. Highdive was letting him take the Enforcer role this time and that meant he would be responsible for any physical shows of force. As a new Brother he would normally not even be involved in something like this except as backup. Dragon appreciated the respect they were giving him because of the harm done to his woman. Any action he took had to be swift and brutal in order to keep things from escalating because even an amateur could get in a lucky shot if things went south.

The four of them pulled into the lot and found what they expected. Twenty guys, half probably under the age of 21, all trying their best to look tough.

The four Dark Sons parked and turned off their bikes. Without a word, they dismounted and let Hawk take the lead. Dragon saw Tico back away from the group towards the car Sharp had indicated held a hostage. It took all his self-control not to pull his gun and kill the fucker for what he had done to Tari.

'*I've got Tico in sites*' Rooster's hushed voice came over the coms.

'*No sign of Chobo*' Grinder added.

Hawk stopped about 30 feet from Diablo and crossed his arms. Dragon, Max and Highdive positioned themselves behind him so they could get clear shots if needed.

"*Amigo.*" Diablo spread his arms as if welcoming them. "I was expecting you to bring more of your men. Word on the street is you aren't pleased about the little misunderstanding that happened last week."

Though his words were friendly, Dragon noticed he didn't step out from his men. Hawk remained silent for uncomfortable seconds before speaking.

"Misunderstanding?"

Diablo chuckled and slapped his thighs as if brushing off dirt. "You should have told us one of your men's baby momma was working for us. The puta running our distribution shop tried to blame her for the mess with the cops. Had we known she was Sharp's, we would have handled things differently."

Dragon had suspected Diablo might be out of the loop on

some things but it sounded like he had been fed a complete fairytale.

"Where's Chobo?" Hawk's tone could have dropped the temperature several degrees.

"Now, Hawk, you don't expect me to hand over one of my men because he got a little rough with a woman." Diablo gestured back behind him. "I've brought the bitch who lied to us and caused this mess. You can hardly blame Chobo for lashing out. The police raid cost us a lot of product." A slight tinge of fear now colored Diablo's voice. He gestured to his men probably to go get the woman he hoped would pacify Hawk.

The sound of a car door opening was followed by a gunshot. Dragon's muscles tensed and he scanned the area for danger.

'*Tico shot the hostage. Orders?*' Rooster's voice was empty as he probably sited down the man.

Like idiot bystanders, every one of the Jacks had spun to see what happened. Tico scrambled to get into the driver's seat of one of the cars followed by the sound of an engine turning over violently. He reached to close the car door.

"Rooster, disable. Grinder, engine block." Hawk's voice was calm as if commenting on the weather. Within five seconds three gunshots echoed through the parking lot. Tico was screaming, the car had stalled and there were two smoking holes in the hood of the car. Dragon held steady, only years of discipline had him waiting for an order rather than moving. Hawk tilted his head slightly towards him. "Bring me Tico, alive."

Two of the Jacks had run over to Tico and were trying to help him with the gaping hole he now had in his left calf. Dragon strode over, ignoring the pulled guns the gangbangers held gripped in shaking hands. When he reached to drag Tico by the arm out of the car the two morons who had been trying to help their friend tried to stop him. Dragon grabbed the first by the back of his skull and slammed him face first into the back-door hearing bone and glass crunch. Using a side kick he took out the second man's knee then brought an elbow around and caught the gangbanger in the temple. A knife to the throat finished the job.

Dragon enjoyed the screams of pain from Tico as he easily dragged him across the pavement. It was almost humorous, the ridiculous reactions on the lower-level Jacks' faces, their jaws dropped and eyes wide. Not one of these boys had ever faced off against real danger. They were used to being bullies and had no idea how to react. Dragon tossed Tico to the ground in front of Hawk resisting the urge to kick him in the head. The action seemed to free some of the gang from shock and several pulled out their guns from their waistbands.

"You might want to tell your boys to ease down if they hope to survive this meeting." Max's voice held a sick, teasing humor; as if he hoped they wouldn't and he might be able to kill someone.

"Put your guns down, idiots!" Diablo shouted. "What the fuck is going on here?" The Jacks' leader looked like he was about to lose his shit and attack someone, but one look at Hawk's impressively scary face had him easing back.

"Highdive give him the folder." Highdive didn't hesitate in responding to Hawk's order. He jogged back to his bike and pulled out the packet of information Tek had pulled together for just this purpose. Returning to the group, that now had a sobbing Tico in the middle, he tossed the large envelope to Diablo.

The man clutched the package but didn't move to open it. "What game are you playing, Hawk? Who shot, Tico?"

"Is that what you think this is, Diablo, a fucking game?" The way Hawk said Diablo he might as well have been saying piece of shit. "Was it a game when your boy sold your poison out of my business?"

Diablo was shaking his head and looked ready to piss himself. "No, we moved our—"

Hawk cut him off. "How about when they got into bed with slavers and sold children to sicko pedophiles, again on my fucking property?"

"We never had the younger kids at the spa," Tico whined from the ground.

Hawk continued as if he hadn't heard. "Or when they attacked a woman under Dark Son protection... twice after they damn well knew she was ours because there were three Brothers with her."

"What the fuck?" Diablo sputtered.

"Flak, bring the van," Hawk said quietly and the squeal of tires from a block away was the evidence the prospect heard. "Evidence is in your hands. Oh, and it wasn't cops that got your product. You have twenty-four hours to deliver Chobo or we go to war."

Flak pulled up at speed and the side door swung open revealing Clean and three other Brothers in full tactical gear and fully automatic weapons. They poured out of the van as Max and Highdive picked up and tossed Tico in. The men retreated back in the Van and sped away.

The whole action took about a minute but none of the Jacks moved. Hawk turned with Dragon, Highdive, and Max following him back to their bikes.

"What do you mean the cops don't have our product?" Diablo shouted finally, coming out of his daze.

Hawk kick-started his bike. "Twenty-four hours."

Chapter 28

I'm not a voyeur, I'm an enthusiastic bystander.

ari woke to the sound of music thumping through the walls and the overwhelming urge to pee. She looked around the room and was disappointed to see Dragon hadn't yet returned. Her muscles ached, she wanted to roll over and go back to sleep since her mind was foggy from fatigue, but her bladder was insistent.

Stumbling out of bed, she steadied herself against the wall, cursing how uncoordinated she felt. It was only after she managed to walk down the hall and find a bathroom, that she fully woke up. She stared at her reflection in the mirror. The healing cuts that ran from the base of her neck were just visible in the men's t-shirt she wore.

The bruising on her face was barely noticeable anymore, giving her hope that physically she would eventually heal. With the memories of the attack restored, she knew she had been lucky to survive. The thought that those two men were still out there and wanted her dead was terrifying. Although it went against her usual philosophy, she secretly hoped Dragon and his Brothers would make them feel as helpless as she had felt.

Tari heard voices outside the bathroom, making her realize she was in a building full of strange men, and she had wandered out in nothing but Dragon's shirt. From the loud music and hum of voices she was pretty sure there was a party going on downstairs. She hoped she could make it back to the bedroom without anyone seeing her, but was determined to brazen it out if she was caught.

She opened the door, taking a glance down the hallway. No one was visible so she tried to move quickly back towards her room. A few doors down, Tari heard a woman's moan and froze. A red door, three down from the room she was staying in, was wide open.

Her mind flashed back to Dragon's earlier explanations. Red doors were party rooms. The door being open meant the occupants wanted company. How many people were already in there? She shouldn't look in, shouldn't stop and watch. She should walk by quickly and get back into bed before anyone saw her in the short shirt that barely covered her ass.

Her breath sped up as she heard a masculine growl filled with lust. Just a peek as she walked by wouldn't hurt anyone. If they had wanted privacy they would have closed the door. She would look, then hurry back to bed. No one would ever know she had been there.

Tari crept forward, fully intent on catching only a glimpse, but the scene inside the room had her steps faltering and her pussy tightening. A brunette woman had her wrists bound above her head to some sort of chain that hung from the ceiling. Head thrown back in obvious pleasure, she was naked except for a ball gag and a harness that crisscrossed her body but covered nothing. Two gorgeous, shirtless men bracketed her like a vision of dark and light.

She had met Hannibal and Ink during her time in the hospital. The vision of the Hot Texas charmer and sultry Louisiana seducer focused on the bound woman had Tari wet in an instant. Ink was lightly but expertly whipping the girl's pussy with a flogger that looked like it was well and often used. Hannibal was clamping her nipples with a silver chain attached that glittered in the low light of the room and shook with every blow.

The woman's moans of pleasure, along with the soft thudding of the flogger had Tari's knees weakening and she stumbled a little forward. She caught herself on the door jamb and her cheeks flushed when Ink caught her eye. His wink had her breath catching. Never before had someone known she was watching them in such an intimate moment. The idea aroused her and she wished Dragon was here. Hannibal turned his head and the small, sexy smile he gave her had probably melted hundreds of women's panties and, if she had been wearing any, her's would have probably combusted.

Tari knew she should walk away, but when both men stripped off their pants in motions that appeared almost choreographed her body just wouldn't comply. They rolled on condoms while the woman's muffled begging filled the room. Though neither man now looked at her, the knowledge they both knew she was watching had her nipples painfully hard.

Hannibal stepped forward, sliding his cock between the woman's thighs, lifting her so her legs wrapped around his hips. Her moan of pleasure was beautiful, as the big man slipped inside her. Ink stepped up behind the woman, her scream primal as he thrust forward, telling Tari exactly what he had done. The two men were like machines and the woman was obviously loving having them stuffed deep inside her.

Tari stepped back intending to finally flee, but found herself bumping against a wall of solid muscle. She would have screamed but a hand wrapped around her mouth muffling any sound. Strong arms closed around her, dragging her down the hall and into a room so quickly she didn't even struggle.

"What the fuck, *Mami*? I'm gone for a few hours and you go looking for some other man?" The sound of Dragon's voice settled her a bit as he put her down on the bed of the room she had been sleeping in. He forced her legs apart, and she felt her sex dripping in the open air. Whatever response she was going to make was cut off by a yelp as he slapped the skin right over her clit.

Pleasure chased the pain in a confusing rush and her body heated. A second wet slap had her groaning and tossing her head back. After she arched up into the fifth strike, his powerful hands flipped her over onto her stomach. The fabric of the sheet caressed up her body as he jerked her down to the end of the mattress. Her legs touched the floor, and she tried to stand and explain herself.

"*Papi*, I wasn't—"

The sharp spank cut off her words. He pushed her back over the mattress. Embarrassment and excitement heated her cheeks. His growls as he slapped the back of her thighs, sent chills up her spine. She didn't want Dragon to think she had been cheating on him, but he wasn't letting her explain.

"Were you standing in the hallway with your pussy barely covered?"

His sharp blows against her ass were having a confusing effect on her body and mind. With every new streak of pain her mind cleared, but between each blow her excitement grew and muddled her thoughts with nothing but desire.

Coming up with a quick, coherent answer was almost impossible.

"Yes, but–"

"Were you standing in the doorway of a red room? A room, I specifically told you, is for my Brothers who like to share and invite others in."

His next blow was sharp against her sit spot and she tried to wiggle away but he held her still. She squirmed under the next few blows before huffing out her required answer.

"Yes."

Rough hands kneaded her ass. The mixture of warmth and pain tightening her nipples and sending her excitement dripping down her thighs. "Ten more, *Mami*. That is your punishment. Then I'm going to show you you don't need to go anywhere but to me to satisfy any needs you may have. Can you take ten more for me?"

Her body ached almost as much from desire as it did from pain. Tari knew she shouldn't have paused at that door. She knew she shouldn't have watched the erotic activities inside. If her actions made Dragon doubt her commitment to them, she deserved any punishment that came her way. She gripped the bedspread and nodded.

"No, *mi reina*." His hand brushed over her reddened flesh in teasing strokes. "I want to hear you say it. Say, You can punish me, *Papi*."

Why did his words turn her on so much? She shivered under his touch, needing him in a way she had never thought possible. "You can punish me, *Papi*."

Time blurred as each stoke lit up her ass with a heat and intensity that was overwhelming. After the last stroke, Dragon flipped her back onto her back and he spread her legs wide. The sheet was rough against her sensitized skin. She moaned as he ran his fingers through her excitement, barely brushing her clit.

"I don't think that was a punishment for my dirty girl."

He thrust two fingers deep inside her pussy in an almost brutal stroke. His frustration radiated from him as he thrust deep and fast, working her clit with his thumb until she thrashed, screaming. She wanted to protest, but her mind shattered as she orgasmed. It was painfully quick, and he didn't let up on his thrusts. He continued circling her clit, speeding up his rhythm and forced a second wave of painful pleasure, then a third, from her writhing body.

Tari caught her breath. Never had she had orgasms ripped out of her body with no recovery time. He ripped open his jeans, not bothering to get undressed. His rigid cock was a thing of beauty and even though she was wrung out, she couldn't wait to feel it insider her. Dragon savagely pulled her almost off the edge of the bed and slammed himself deep in one quick stroke.

Like a man possessed, he slammed back in with what had to be all of his strength bottoming out and building another impossible orgasm deep within her.

"Who does this pussy belong to, *Mami*?" He continued pounding, forcing her to open around him even as she trembled into another orgasm.

"You, *Papi!* I'm all yours, Dragon." She screamed out another orgasm and felt Dragon follow her over the edge with a shout of his own as his cum spilled out. His body seemed to deflate losing the hot edge of rage that had driven him.

He rested his forehead against hers as if trying to get his breathing under control.

Tari reached up and ran her hand down Dragon's cheek. Her body was limp and sore from the mind-blowing orgasms she had just experienced. She had heard women brag about the intensity of angry sex but, until now, had never experienced it firsthand. She felt guilty for being the cause of such anger but fully understood why some women might taunt their men if it led to sex like that.

She almost giggled when she realized he was still fully dressed and yet still deep inside her. One look at his face killed that urge. The anger was melting away to be replaced by hurt that tore at her heart.

"I wasn't looking for another man. I wouldn't have cheated on you."

He pulled out of her and she missed the intimacy immediately. Pulling her up he sat next to her on the bed, his eyes searching her face.

"Explain it to me, *Mami*, because finding you dressed like that in that doorway." Dragon sighed "It pissed me off."

The truth was embarrassing but Tari knew she would have to share it all. "I got up to use the restroom and didn't think to put on pants. On my way back that door was open."

"And you just had to stop in?" Dragon's voice verged on mocking, but Tari chose to ignore it understanding how ridiculous it sounded.

Now she could embarrass herself completely and hope he would understand, or keep quiet, and he would always think she might have cheated if he hadn't come by in time. She fought with the urge to cover up and not be as vulnerable as she shared this secret part of herself. "Do you have a kink?" The words were the only way she could think of easing into the conversation but the surprised look on his face was adorable.

"Two men is your kink?"

Tari quickly shook her head. "No. But do you have a kink? Something outside the normal that gets you hard if you even think about it."

"Not like whips, or chains, or anything."

"Fine. Something that you fantasize about then?"

Dragon gave her a dirty grin. "I have many fantasies, but I

love your long legs." He ran a hand up her thigh. "That first night when you bent yourself in half and those gorgeous legs and ass were on display. I jacked off many nights to that image when I was overseas."

Now they were getting somewhere. She remembered that night vividly. "What else do you want to do to me?"

"I want to fuck you standing up from behind. I'm too tall usually to do that but you, *mi reina* are the perfect height for me to slide right in and fuck you hard." The image had her shivering and arousal spooling back up even though they had just finished. Sharp gave her thigh a sharp smack dragging her back from the daydream. "What does this have to do with why you were at that door?"

"I like to watch." She held her breath not sure how much he wanted to hear.

"People fucking?" His tone was interested without the judgement she feared.

"Everything. The sight, the sounds, all of it. I don't need it to get off, but I can admit not being able to resist if it is right there in front of me. When I walked by and saw Hannibal and Ink with that woman…"

The memory of what she had seen filled her mind's eye and she took a deep breath. Pain clutched her head and the memory started blurring into another one.

Tari pulled back the curtain, terror and excitement causing her hand to shake. She couldn't believe she would be seeing Dragon after all this time. Would he even remember her? The night they had together changed her life in so many ways but at best he would think she had ghosted him.

She had stepped halfway past the divider when a deep voice tinged with a Louisiana bayou accent spoke. "Now that is a lovely sight."

Tari had to stop moving or step into a gorgeous blonde woman who was in the process of dropping her dress to the floor. Her hands running over her body that was obviously sculpted by exercise and a plastic surgeon's knife.

"I can't help myself." The woman's voice was deep and airy like a phone sex operator. *"The thought of you two touching me, filling me, always makes me impatient."*

"My hands are busy right now but feel free to get yourself ready." Hannibal groaned and Tari couldn't blame him, the sight of the woman working her body while they watched was breathtaking.

Walking in on this scene was the last thing she expected but she couldn't seem to back away, the sight and sounds the woman was making were hypnotic.

"Cristo." A voice she hadn't heard in years came from the chair in front of the woman. *"How much longer?"*

Her ears rang and she couldn't make out the words that followed. Laying down flat on the chair was Dragon, her Dragon, and he was getting ready to fuck this bimbo with the man currently giving him a tattoo. Shame and humiliation flooded her system erasing her arousal and she turned and fled.

"Tari, what's wrong?" Dragon was shaking her shoulders lightly, but she felt like the whole world was upside down.

Her mind was still fuzzy, and she knew getting out what she had to in English would be too slow so she chose Spanish to vent her confusion. *"I thought you said you didn't share your women."*

"What are you talking about?"

"The blonde woman you and Hannibal shared. I remember watching her get ready for you."

"Madre de Cristo." Dragon stood up, zipping himself back into his pants, and stormed out of the room. Tari was scared he didn't plan on coming back. What about her question made him run away?

A minute later Dragon dragged a half-dressed, laughing Hannibal into the room.

"Hello again, *Cher*." Hannibal's French endearment caught her off guard and she blushed. "To what do I owe this abrupt invitation to your room?"

Tari grabbed the edge of the comforter and used it to cover her half naked state. Crazy thoughts swirled through her mind. She didn't want to have sex with anyone but Dragon. Why had he brought this man fresh from fucking another woman to their room? A soft laugh from the doorway told Tari her humiliation was complete. Ink was watching them with an amused smirk.

"Have I ever shared a woman with you?" Dragon's anger tinged his words.

"No. And if you're offering, as you saw, my dance card is already full tonight."

"Tari remembered seeing Didi when you were finishing my tat at the shop."

"No worries, lovely. Your man is pure of that particular sin," Ink's smooth drawl added from the doorway.

Tari didn't know what to say, so she nodded, hoping the floor would open and swallow her whole. Thankfully, Hannibal rolled his eyes and left along with his partner in crime.

"You could have just said so. I would have believed you," Tari mumbled, looking down at her lap.

Dragon stepped close and cupped her face, so she had to look up at him. "Maybe. But now you know. The only other memory with me in it should be me chasing you down to Traker's and explaining just that. Then I dragged you to the back room and, after I finally got a small taste of you, you sent me away."

A tear slipped down her cheek and Dragon brushed it away with his thumb. "I don't know what to say."

"You are mine, Tari, no sharing, but if you like to watch I have plenty of Brothers who like to put on a show. I will get you so worked up you'll be begging for me to fuck you wherever we are. You want my fantasy, that's it. My dirty queen with my patch on her back begging to be fucked. So horny she doesn't care where we are or who is around."

His words sent fire straight from her heart to her core. It was a little twisted, but his dirty words meant so much more to her. He might not have said he loved her, but she had no doubt that she had fallen deeply and irreversibly in love with him.

Chapter 29

Sometimes it is the family you choose that matters.

Tari's dreams had been filled with returning memories. She should have been exhausted after Dragon had spent most of the night proving he could play her body like a concert pianist, but instead she woke up fresh. He seemed reluctant earlier when he left her side, saying he had to review the books of several of the Club's smaller businesses. Unable to just sit in this room waiting, she headed downstairs soon after he left. After seeing several men and their women passed out from a night of partying, she made her way outside.

Though she was nowhere near ready to start her usual yoga routine, Tari decided meditating in the cool fall weather was just what she needed. The view from the backyard of the Dark Sons' Clubhouse was a strange mix of sights. There were a large number of picnic tables and fire pits, utilitarian buildings, old style houses, and a very modern playground off to one side. Beyond it all were majestic trees and, rising above them in the distance, the Colorado Mountains that always called to a part of her soul.

Around the side of the Clubhouse, was a spot of lush grass that gave her a wonderful view that included nothing made by man. It had been years since she had had the opportunity to escape the city completely, and Tari was going to take full advantage. She knelt down and slowed her breathing letting the stress of the past weeks flow out of her and into the universe. Focusing only on the gentle rhythm of her heartbeat, and the brisk breezes of morning air let her swirling thoughts settle into something she could manage.

Life for the last two years had been an uphill struggle with events coming at her so fast there had been little time to do more than react. Although Dragon returning to her life had sent things into overdrive, he had also given her a much-needed strength to find her center again. She loved him. That single truth should make all other choices easy except that being with him meant becoming a part of the Dark Sons.

She had grown up in a closed community that appeared from the outside to be a loving and good place. But from the inside it had been a stifling judgmental prison that had crushed so many souls. The Dark Sons Brothers appeared on the outside to be good if somewhat untraditional. Would staying with Dragon mean segregating herself and her daughter in a dangerous and uncertain lifestyle? She needed to know more before she decided.

No matter how her heart ached at the thought of not being with Dragon, her love and devotion to their daughter had to come first. Maybe talking to Val or Pixie would help her understand better what staying with Dragon would mean.

"I should have known we would find you out here soakin' up the sun like a flower." As if her thoughts had summoned her, Val walked around the Clubhouse and toward her with Citlali toddling at her side.

"Mama!"

Val's southern twang along with the cheerful greeting of her daughter drew Tari peacefully from her inner meditations. She turned to watch her daughter waddle on tiny legs toward her at top speed. The world held many beautiful things in it but none of them compared to joy on a child's face. Lali was dressed in a cute, tiny yellow dress with matching leggings and hairband holding back her silky black hair. Tari held out her arms expecting to be tackled by an enthusiastic hug.

The little girl stumbled to a stop a few feet from her mother and clapped her hands together in an adorable bowing gesture. "Namate Mama."

When had she learned that? Had she taught her? Trying to get her, once again, whirling emotions under control Tari copied her gesture and said, "Namaste Lali girl."

She pulled her daughter in for a kiss and let her smooth skin and fresh scent soothe her jangled nerves.

"Oh, isn't that just precious." Val smiled then caught sight of the prospect standing by the Clubhouse door. "Flak, you on Tari duty?"

Tari hadn't been happy when Dragon had said she was going to have someone assigned to watch over her if he wasn't around, but she understood he had business to take care of this morning, and hadn't wanted to be cooped up in a room watching him read over books. So far the prospect had stayed unobtrusive allowing her, at least, the illusion of being alone.

"That would be me." He smiled and it looked good on his dark, rough features. The man had nothing on Dragon's regal Mezzo American looks but she might be a bit biased.

"We got a little one out here and Cheryl is bringing over her girls as well, so you make sure none of the leftovers wander out back, ya here?"

He smirked and nodded his agreement.

"Leftovers?" Tari watched her daughter wander off a bit towards some late season dandelion flowers.

"The women not yet thrown out the door. Sometimes they wander about like the party is still going on. You can get an eyeful you just can't wash away with bleach."

"Maybe we should go somewhere else." Lali was too young to really understand or care about much, but Tari didn't want her exposed to things like that.

"Don't you fuss. Flak will do his job. We usually keep the kids away from the Clubhouse except on family days and the boys know to keep their pets from roaming outside the Clubhouse."

Tari had to laugh. "You don't think much of those women do you?"

"Some of them are just fine, but a rotten whore can just up and spoil the bushel."

"Val!" Tari was taken aback a bit by the blatant rudeness from the woman who always hid her insults in funny sayings. The southern woman burst out in laughter when she saw the shocked look on Tari's face. And that set the two of them laughing. They let the laughter fade to smiles as they pulled themselves together.

"You're sounding better today. Doesn't sound like you're struggling with your words."

"The therapist said the better rested and less stressed I am, the easier it should be."

"Well we will have to make sure you find your Zen."

Pixie and a woman Tari didn't know came around the side of the building. Pixie was decked out in a white maternity sundress with splotches of color sprinkled cutely across the fabric paired with the Dark Sons vest. The woman she walked with was elegant beauty with long, black hair much like Tari's own but an Indian cast to her skin and features. Two little girls trailed behind her: one looked only slightly older than her own Lali and the other she guessed to be around six. Both girls shared their mother's beauty but where she was dressed in a sleek set of black jeans and black turtleneck they had princess costumes billowing around them in the breeze.

Tari guessed this was Cheryl and when the woman got close enough she saw the woman wore the same black leather vest that Val and Pixie wore but with the name Deep next to the property patch.

"What's so funny?" Tari recognized the voice of the woman from the phone call at the hospital and remembered she had also called the lawyer on the phone Cheryl.

Val smiled down at Tari who finally stood not wanting to be kneeling on the ground when everyone else was standing. "I was just commenting on the facts of Club life and shocking poor Tari."

Cheryl smiled in greeting. "Ah the traditional induction of the innocent. Hi, I'm Cheryl. It's nice to finally meet you in person. These are my girls, Sasha is the little one and Ava."

"Nice to meet you all." Tari's daughter toddled back over and clutched onto her mother's legs. "This is Citlali but I usually just call her Lali."

Lali held out a handful of stems to the little girls which had probably been dandelions before being stripped by small hands. "Fowers."

Sasha smiled and looked up at her mother. "Can we go pick flowers too?"

"Sure, honey." Cheryl smiled watching the girls run off to start picking the tiny wildflowers growing nearby.

The sight of the three little girls together was heartwarming. Tari had never had the time or money to get Lali into any playgroups so she could meet and socialize with other kids. How many children came around the compound? Val had mentioned family days but how many of these outwardly rough men had small children?

"Ready to see your new place?" Pixie smiled brightly gesturing to a two-story building across the field.

"My new place?" Tari was confused. She knew Dragon's mother had been watching Lali at his place while she was in the hospital but why would they be calling it her place?

Cheryl smiled. "The boys got all your stuff moved into one of the open two-bedroom apartments. They didn't think it was safe to leave your stuff in that neighborhood with the window broken and wanted you to have a safe place to stay while you recovered."

Tears pricked at the edge of her eyes. Pride wanted to rear its ugly head and tell her to refuse but honestly what other option did she have? "I didn't know. Dragon didn't mention anything."

"Sure as cornbread goes with greens I swear men can only operate one head at a time." Val reached out and squeezed Tari's hand gently. "Darlin', I promise me and the girls made sure the men set it up right for a little one who might get into things. Let's go get some of your stuff settled in so you feel at home."

Chapter 30

Target Acquired.

L ooking over the books was the last thing Dragon
wanted to be doing. Tari had woken up with nightmares several times last night, and by morning he
was ready to rip apart the world to find Chobo and make
him suffer. Giving up, he slammed the account book
closed.

He strode out of the office he was using and over to
Hawk's office. The door was open showing his President
sitting with Tek deep in discussion. Hawk looked up with a
grim expression. "You should hear this, Brother." He gestured
to a seat making Dragon's stomach lurch. What more could
have gone wrong?

Hawk nodded to Tek who began speaking, "Diablo
contacted us early this morning with Chobo's location."

Rage burned across Dragon's skin. "Why wasn't I told?"

"He was already dead," Hawk broke in. "I made the call

to send over some Brothers to check it out before you were told."

Dragon took a deep breath trying to swallow the anger, but his throat convulsed and his muscles wouldn't loosen. "Who killed him?" He wanted the name of the asshole who had stolen his vengeance.

Tek shook his head. "We don't know. But whoever it was, tortured him for a long time."

That satisfied a small part of the rage burning inside him but brought up so many more questions. "Were they trying to get information?"

"Possibly. But his tongue was cut out and every finger removed. The torture was thorough." Tek smiled and Dragon thought his Brother shared his righteous anger.

Hawk leaned back in his chair. The President's face giving nothing away. "The Jacks might beat a man to death or shoot him but this wasn't their style."

"So, do you think this has to do with the drugs or the girls we found?" If it was the drugs, Tari might still be in danger but Dragon knew she had never been involved with the other.

Tek shrugged. "We're looking into it. Cartels can get this vicious, but they would have gone after more than just Chobo. Right now, my money is on the Russians. Eastern European girls and we just found a money trail from some of the guys we killed at the house."

Hawk caught Dragon's gaze. "It's more than just money. Those guys at the house should have been in jail a long time ago, but somehow each one of them always got off on a technicality. Missing evidence, bad procedure, or a deal that should never have been offered."

"You're thinking dirty cops?" The thought didn't surprise Dragon. The profession called out to the best and worst men for drastically different reasons. Something was bothering him, something he should remember. "Fuck! Volker. That asshole cornered Tari when she was in the hospital. I thought it was because we got him busted down but what if–"

"Master V," Hawk's angry voice cut in. "Son of a bitch was in with that asshole who kidnapped Pixie."

Tek pulled out his phone and started typing. "I moved the Ukrainian girls to a safehouse out of state while we were figuring out a safe new home for them. I'll get a photo of Volker to the woman I have watching them so we can confirm."

Hawk leaned forward putting his elbows on his knees. "Volker doesn't have the stones to do what was done to Chobo. If it is the Russians, who are we dealing with and what is their next move?"

Dragon had no experience with enemy actions outside of insurgents but he tried to piece things together. "For the Russians this is business. So they are either going to want money, their girls, or some form of compensation."

"Girls are off the table," Tek snapped and Hawk nodded.

"Everything is off the table for now. This whole thing could be over as far as they are concerned."

Dragon glared at Hawk. "This isn't over for me. If Volker had anything to do with what happened to Tari, I'm going to beat him to death with my own hands." The two men locked eyes for a full minute. Hawk nodded and Dragon knew he would have whatever support he needed to make that man pay.

Hawk stood and walked toward his desk. "Your woman needs to stay locked down until we figure this shit out. You putting your patch on her back?"

"Yeah."

"Damn." Tek chuckled. "Never imagined a yoga instructor as an Old Lady."

Dragon raised an eyebrow. "But a 1%er biker who is CEO of a billion-dollar Tech company is perfectly normal, right?"

Tek shrugged. "I'll get a welcome package together for her. Cut, phone, and jewelry all with GPS tracking. What kind of jewelry will she wear every day?"

"Not sure she'll go for being tracked." His woman was a free spirit and would probably balk at being tracked like that.

Hawk sat down behind his desk. "Not a negotiation. You don't share details with your woman or any man outside of Officers. It's Club business to keep our families safe."

Dragon understood what he was being told and nodded his acceptance. He thought about Tek's question. "A charm bracelet." His mother wore hers every day with mementos of a full life out on display. Tari wouldn't want flashy jewelry so if he wanted any chance of her wearing it every day it had to be sentimental.

"Easy enough. What name do you want on her patch?"

Everyone in the Dark Sons had a road name including the Old Ladies. Not all of them used it but it was on their cut. Dragon flipped through possibilities in his mind before smiling. "*Reina*. She is my Queen."

Chapter 31

Girls talk to each other like men talk to each other. But girls have an eye for detail -Amy Winehouse

The walk over to the apartment complex was brutal on Tari's shaking legs. She was glad for the excuse of the toddlers' smaller legs to take her time. Sasha and Lali had bonded immediately and tried to pick every wildflower they stumbled across while Ava watched over them. By the time they reached the door of the apartment the three girls were dirty with arms full of weeds.

Tari was proud she had made it all the way without stopping, but practically fell into the first chair she found. The apartment was much bigger and nicer than she had expected. She sat in a living room roughly the size of her studio apartment. A kitchen and hallway were visible from her chair and she expected the bedrooms were down the hallway. Pixie took the girls down the hall and set them up with snacks and a Princess movie in what was now Lali's room.

Boxes lined one wall of the living room that she hoped contained all her stuff. There were no decorations or personal touches anywhere. The furniture was nice if not exactly brand-new reminding Tari of the dorms where she had gone to college. Everything was moving so fast. She wasn't sure if she should treat this place like their new home or just a temporary stop while she got back on her feet.

"This place is nicer than I expected. Do all the Brothers live in these apartments?" Tari was grateful for a place to stay but wondered what living surrounded by bikers would be like.

"Worried about being kept up all night by raging parties?" Cheryl cut right to the heart of her concerns.

"A bit." Tari laughed.

Val chuckled and sat next to her. "Only about half of the twenty-four apartments have someone living in them and about half of those are Brothers on deployment so they aren't here much. Your next-door neighbor is Marjorie and her cuter than a June bug son Dylan. I think he is a year or two older than little Lali. Marjorie is a widow from the Texas chapter who moved here a few months ago for a new start."

"Widow?" Was it wrong that her mind went right to the worst place? How dangerous was the Biker life?

"Sad story that. It's all romantic that making a woman an Old Lady means more to the men than marriage vows but a piece of paper would have made that woman's life so much easier." Cheryl shook her head. "Army doesn't recognize a patch on a woman's back so the only benefits she gets is for the boy. She's lucky Dark Sons take care of their own or she'd be struggling trying to make ends meet and taking care of that child alone."

Tari was glad her dark complexion hid her blush. She was all too aware of how hard it was to struggle by yourself as a single mom. "You guys took her in?"

"She got accepted to a program in Denver. Hawk invited

her to live here and cover her costs till she's back on her feet." Pixie's voice overflowed with the pride that those honorable actions deserved.

Tari thought back to her own childhood. One summer when they were staying in a compound between missionary trips one of the men had died in a car crash. His wife and children had been moved out of their house and into the dorms almost immediately to make a place for a younger married couple. She had asked about her and was told that the woman would probably be made a second wife to someone if she couldn't tempt one of the single men into taking on her and her children. They hadn't been at risk of starving but since the woman didn't have any skills other than being a mother she wasn't valued. That, along with so many other things, had solidified Tari's desire to break away from the restrictive lifestyle.

"That is pretty amazing. I didn't mean to sound ungrateful for everything you all have done. Last night's party sounded pretty wild and I have Lali to think about." She wanted these ladies to know she wasn't trying to judge them or this lifestyle but wasn't sure how to voice all her concerns. Not just for today but the future.

"Oh those boys know to keep their shenanigans to the Clubhouse, and not let anyone but family wander deeper into the compound. I like to think of this place as an untraditional gated community." Val's laugh was comforting. "There are about sixteen houses beyond the tree line. Most are near each other for those that are more settled and want their own places and about half the Brothers live in Denver to be closer to work or family."

"I know Deep and I are thinking about building on property now that Sasha is school age. The community school here is so much better, and it would be nice knowing you all are here if I ever needed back up with the kids." Cheryl winked at Pixie and Val.

"That would be amazing!" Pixie clapped her hands with enthusiasm.

"I feel like I'm in the twilight zone. Had someone asked me to describe what living in a Biker compound was like it would not have included playgrounds and gated communities."

"Oh, Darlin. Dark Sons, especially here in Denver, are not what you would consider typical by any means. Our men work, fight, and fuck hard and dirty. They aren't always on the legal side of the law but with all my heart I believe they are always on the right side. It's not a lifestyle for the faint of heart and it is not always an easy path being different from the mainstream." Val's words held a passion that reminded her of some of the true believers she grew up with.

"I grew up in a closed religious community, that was so far away from the mainstream, I rarely ever saw anyone who wasn't part of it or being preached to by it. My mother couldn't have children, so she adopted me in order to save my soul and show what a good Christian woman she was. It wasn't an abusive household, just a cold and isolating one. I don't want that for Lali."

"Do you miss your parents?" Pixie asked.

"Yes and no. I think every child wants their parents to love and cherish them but I accepted long ago that I was never going to be what my parents wanted."

"All I want for my baby is for him or her to be happy." Pixie rubbed her small belly with a sad smile on her face.

"Can I ask you ladies a question?" Tari knew so little about being part of the biker life that wasn't found somewhere in fiction and she trusted these women to give her the unvarnished truth.

Cheryl sat down in another chair. "Of course."

Pixie and Val settled on the couch while Tari sorted through the questions she had, deciding on the most important. "Dragon said he wants to see his Patch on my back." Pixie squealed, clapping her hands and Tari smiled. "Does that mean he wants me to be his 'Old Lady'?"

"Yes! Only a man's Old Lady can wear his Patch. Did he give you a cut?" Pixie was practically bouncing off her chair.

"Cut?" The word was familiar but Tari couldn't remember what it was.

Cheryl gestured to the black leather vest that both her and Pixie wore. "They call this vest a cut when it has MC patches on it." She turned around showing that sewed onto the back was a beautiful Patch with the Dark Sons' logo and the words Property of Deep underneath.

Tari noticed Val wasn't wearing one. "You don't have one, Val?"

Val threw back her head and laughed. "Oh Lord, yes I do, but I only wear it if I'm going outside the compound or I'm going to be around people who aren't family. Ain't no one here that doesn't know who I am or who they will be answering to if they disrespect me."

The phrasing was odd, but Tari liked that these women openly announced their relationships and allegiances to the outside world. There was an honesty in the whole set up that appealed to her. "What does it mean to be an Old Lady?"

Cheryl and Pixie both looked to Val which was odd to Tari since Cheryl looked to be the oldest but there must be more to the social structure than just age.

"It is slightly different for each couple, but like a marriage there are some basic expectations. Something you need to accept before ever putting on that Patch is that his Brothers will always come first."

"And that will never change. Deep missed Ava's first dance recital with no more explanation then," Cheryl made her voice low and gravely, "Club business, Babe." She smiled a little. "I was so angry but when my little girl danced out onto stage eight big burly men stood up in the back of the auditorium and cheered. When she was done, they whistled and hollered her name like she had just won the Super Bowl. Deep had her do her dance for the whole Club at the next Barbeque and she loved every minute of it."

"Did you ever find out why he left?" Tari was amazed at the love, acts like that, displayed.

"Not directly but that was around the time of Pixie's troubles with the cops so I'm guessing it was something to do with that." Cheryl shrugged. "I trust his Brothers wouldn't pull him away for a silly reason, but it still stings sometimes."

"When you take his patch, you don't just get Dragon you get all his Brothers, good and bad. As long as there is a Club member breathing you will never be alone." Val winked at her. "But the MC lifestyle isn't for everyone. We live hard, play hard, and have our men's backs no matter what it costs us. You need to trust and respect your man enough to follow his lead without question in public."

Pixie threw back her head and laughed. "What we say in private is completely up to us."

The idea of loyalty and family fed a lonely part of her soul. She wasn't naive, there was a reason these men lived the way they did, but she knew in her heart Dragon would never hurt her or Citlali. It was hard to imagine but she knew she was ready to take the leap of faith. He was worth it.

"Is there a ceremony? Like a marriage?"

Cheryl gave a chuckling cough. "You could say that."

Val shook her head. "Nothing so formal as that. He has to claim you with at least five Brothers as witnesses and you have to accept his claim." She raised her eyebrows up and down a few times suggestively. "Some people, like Banshee, take that claiming to a new level."

Did claiming mean more than just saying the words? She was almost afraid to ask. "Banshee?" Tari hadn't met anyone with that name.

Pixie started turning the cutest shade of pink. She waved her hand. "That would be me. I might have a bit of a temper at times."

"Really?" Tari was shocked and Val and Cheryl burst out laughing.

"I also might like putting on a show." Pixie gave a wicked smile and Tari was floored. She would have never guessed this sweet looking woman had a dirty side.

"Oh, she likes it like a jackrabbit likes a twitchin' bunny. If you spend any after hours in the Clubhouse main room you will get to see every secret God gave her." The women burst out laughing and Tari could tell that the idea of liking public sex didn't bother any of them. This was just teasing among friends.

The idea of watching Pixie and her man stirred something inside her. Her nipples tightened and her core ached. After seeing what happened in the private rooms the idea of being in a crowded room where lots of people would be letting themselves go was a great temptation. It was Saturday, would there be a party tonight?

"Hola!" Mama Rios's voice interrupted Tari's thoughts.

She stood up and hugged the smaller woman who had just come into the room. "Mama Rios what are you doing here?"

"Mija, your English is much better today."

Tari paused thinking about it. After getting most of her memories back she had only had to focus on her language when stressed. Was it a sign her brain was healing?

"I guess it is."

"What were you ladies laughing about when I came in?" Mama Rios raised an eyebrow as if she somehow knew they had been talking about something dirty.

Tari was stumped at what to say but Pixie came to her rescue. "Dragon told Tari he wanted to make her his Old Lady."

A large smile broke across the older woman's face. "Did you say yes?"

"He didn't actually ask." Tari felt the rightness of everything settle into her stomach and came to a decision. "But if he did, I would say yes." This family, this place was everything she could want for her and Lali. Nothing was perfect but what they had here would make up for any troubles they might face going forward.

Pixie squealed and rushed over to hug her. For a tiny pregnant woman, she had a hell of a grip and Tari had to muffle a groan from the pain of her healing body. The stinging of tears not just from the hug but from all the happy emotions pricked at her eyes. Val, Cheryl, and Mama Rios joined the hug and the warmth and peace was food for her soul.

Mama Rios stepped back with a scowl. "Now, you make sure Gabor understands you deserve a wedding not just some smelly piece of leather." She paused for a second seeming to consider her words then looked at the other women. "Not that your leather vests aren't lovely, ladies."

Val gave a cackle. "Don't you worry, Mama Rios. We all know you love us."

"You should tell him at the party tonight." Pixie was bouncing like a small child who had too much sugar.

Tari shook her head. "I have Lali. I can't go to the party."

"*No seas tonta.* I will take *mi nieta* to my house to give you time to seduce my son into a wedding."

"Mama Rios!" Tari gasped and laughed. Was she being silly? There wasn't any reason to wait and the idea of the wild party was very tempting. For the last two years she hadn't let go and really gotten to enjoy any time as anything but a mother.

"It's settled then." Val gave her a wink.

Pixie giggled. "I have the perfect outfit for you!"

Chapter 32

Using your weakness against you might not be fair but it sure is fun.

The usual chaos that was Saturday night at the Clubhouse held no appeal to Dragon. If Dozer hadn't warned him away, he would have long since left to spend time with Tari. He was glad she was having a good time with some of the Old Ladies. When they came back, he would take that as his cue to leave. Dragon took comfort in the thought his woman had spent the day laughing and making friends rather than being dragged into the muck he was dealing with. Tek had confirmed that Volker was Master V but none of their contacts could get a current location on the man.

Some of those contacts were here right now, getting bribed with free booze and easy pussy to make sure they stayed loyal and motivated. Dragon was sitting off to the side of the room with Max, Sharp, Dozer and Deep while they waited for the Old Ladies to show up. Most of the women who were property only rarely came to parties and would leave early not wanting to deal with how wild it got after the alcohol had been flowing for a while.

Dragon looked at Dozer. "You sure the women coming here tonight is a good idea?" There were a lot more non-Brothers present and from the already barely dressed state of the women, it wouldn't be long before someone was getting fucked or sucked right in the middle of the floor.

"I warned my girl, but do you know what she said?" Dozer took a sip from a bottle of beer, his smile evident even through his beard.

"What?" Val was a crazy wonderful woman who looked out for most of the Old Ladies. But somedays Dragon thought she was more crazy than wonderful.

Dozer chuckled. "She said 'That's perfect'."

"You think they have something planned?" Tari was still healing, excitement was not a good idea. Unless of course it was him doing the exciting.

"My Pixie is with them, so I'm going to guess yes." Sharp laughed.

Dragon looked at Deep. "Cheryl will keep them from going too crazy right?"

Every man at the table let out a bark of laughter. Deep patted him on the shoulder. "Her road name, though she hates it, is Busta." He raised an eyebrow. "As in she can bust a man's nuts in more than just one way. Sorry Brother, but she is more likely to egg them on."

Max gave a low whistle looking across the room. "You fuckers are lucky sons of bitches."

Dragon turned and the sight of the four women stalking towards them had every part of him sitting up and paying attention. Like four goddesses from different pantheons each woman was the very primal expression of sex. Cheryl was sleek and deadly, Val a sparkling vision, and Pixie a slutty school girl. But Tari, Dragon swallowed his groan, was everything he never even knew he wanted.

Thigh high red stiletto boots were visible under a flared black mini skirt that swayed as she walked. A skin tight, concert tee dipped low, hugging her every curve and displaying ebony cleavage that begged for his mouth. Gold framed, her night sky eyes and her lips were a deep color of plum that made them seem impossibly sexier than they usually were. Her long, straight midnight hair was pulled up in a ponytail that had him imagining using it to pull her back as he fucked her from behind.

Val winked at Dozer. "Hey, Sugar. Y'all waiting for us?"

Dragon stood, putting his beer on the table behind him and took the three steps necessary to bring him chest to chest with Tari. He heard, more than saw, his Brothers doing the same with their women.

"*Mi reina*. I have no words." Dragon ran his hand from her hip to her thigh loving how her body shivered. With the boots she was wearing, they were almost eye to eye and he used his other hand to cup her face and draw her in for a kiss.

Her lips parted for him and he didn't hesitate. She tasted like tequila, lime, and pure Tari. Her body pushed against his and her scent filled his nostrils. He groaned into her mouth and pressed his now iron-hard cock against her stomach. He rubbed his cheek against hers and whispered in her ear, "Did you know what this outfit would do to me, *Mami*? What seeing those gorgeous legs in those fuck-me boots would make me want to do?"

The way she bit her lip was adorable. "I plead the fifth."

He chuckled and pulled her a little away from the crowd and the table of his Brothers who were busy greeting their own women in their own ways. There wasn't really anywhere close that they could have real privacy but with a glare he cleared away two hangers-on who were using one of the small pub style tables nearby the wall. He backed her against the wall and ran his hands up her waist using his thumbs to brush up and over her nipples that were now clearly outlined.

"Mmm. So you think you did something wrong?" Dragon nibbled at her ear, enjoying her catching breath.

"No, I just–" She gasped a bit. "I can't think, Dragon, and I have something important to say to you."

Her words gave him pause, fear briefly sending a chill over his skin. He eased up, backing off just a bit. He took another moment to enjoy the perfection that was his woman's body. She wouldn't have worn that sexy as fuck outfit to tell him something bad. "What do you need to tell me?"

"I, uhm, well." Her shoulders and chest rose and fell with a deep breath then another slower one. "Last night. Was amazing."

He smiled, loving every facet of this woman. How she could both be shy, and outgoing was a wonder. She was the whole package whether she was wearing her hippie yoga outfits or this hot as fuck rocker chick look, he wanted her all. "Yes, it was."

"You said something important last night."

"What did I say?" He had said a lot of things last night as he explored every inch of her body.

Tari looked down and it bothered him that she looked so uncomfortable. "That you wanted your patch on my back. *Did you mean it?*"

Dragon didn't think she knew she had slipped into Spanish. He gripped her chin waiting until she looked into his eyes before speaking. "Tari, you are *mi reina*, my queen. I love you and our daughter so much, I hurt when we are apart. I want my patch on your back, my ring on your finger, I want to spend the rest of my life making sure you both know how precious you are to me."

"It's been so quick, it's crazy, but I love you too." She

laughed, the lights dancing in her dark eyes. "Good thing you mentioned a ring cause your mama has definite feelings about that."

Dragon chuckled and moved his grip to cup her face. "I'm sure she does."

"Uhm, so Val said you had to claim me in front of five Brothers. Does that mean what I think?" Dragon felt Tari's cheeks warm.

It was true that five Brothers had to witness the claim and usually it meant exactly what she was asking. He studied her face for how she felt about that. Her eyes were dilated, lips parted. Dragon reached down and ran his hand up under her skirt and found her bare pussy so wet it was almost running down her thigh.

"*Cristo*, you shaved for me, *Mami*?"

Tari nodded and Dragon wanted nothing more than to fuck her right here, but he saw the way she nervously bit her lip. He needed to get her past the fear or drag her upstairs to a private room.

He turned them so the table was between them and the rest of the party. Seeing his Brothers with their own women gave him an idea.

"Turn around, spread your legs, and put your hands on the table."

"You going to frisk me, *Papi*?" Her tone was playful. Dragon raised an eyebrow waiting for her to comply.

She did and his plan almost flew out the window as he took in the sight. It was even better than his fantasies, her luscious ass pushed out her skirt and, if she bent just a little more, he was sure to get a perfect view of her bare pussy.

"Look over at Val." Her head moved slightly. "You see how she's sitting on Dozer's lap. Her shoulders back because he has her arms pinned. I'm betting that under the table he is stroking her little clit. Edging her because he loves driving her to the point of losing control."

Tari's breath was ragged and he could see her thigh muscles clenching. She had said she liked to watch but watching her get worked up had his dick pushing painfully against his zipper. Dragon slipped his hand under her skirt sliding through her wet lips with his fingers till he found the stiff bundle of nerves at her front.

"Can you find Cheryl? Look down at Deep's feet just under the table." He waited till he heard her quick gasp of breath. "See how he grips her hair." Dragon gave a tug on Tari's ponytail. "He's got his cock down her throat, pushing her down on it until she can't breathe. Watch how she struggles."

When Deep let his wife up for air Dragon heard Tari's own gasp and he thrust a finger deep into her tight clutching channel. He added a second finger and her hips bucked back at him trying to force him deeper.

"Dragon." Tari gasped. "Pixie…"

He nipped at her neck grinding against her ass so she could feel what she was doing to him. He looked over and saw Pixie was straddled outward on Sharp's lap. Her top was gone and she was leaning back against her man's chest.

"What do you see, *Mami?*"

He ran his fingers out of her depths and up to the tight ring of muscles on her ass. Using her own honey he circled the area. He was an ass man loving the look of it. He wondered if she would let him claim her fully one day.

She moaned pushing back and he smiled dipping a finger into the forbidden spot just enough to tease.

"Oh God. She's fucking him right at the table. He's pinching her nipples so hard it looks cruel but she is loving it." Tari whimpered and ground back against him, almost making him come in his pants like a teenager.

He started flicking her clit in time with Pixie's up and down rhythm. He needed her so badly If she didn't beg soon he was going to have to take her upstairs.

"Please Papi, I need you inside me. Fuck me please."

Triumph washed across his skin but he needed to be sure. He pressed them chest to back grinding his cock against her as he gave a quick bite on her earlobe.

"I want to Fuck you and make you come so hard every man in this room knows it. Last chance, *Mami*. I can take you upstairs or claim you right here and now with my Brothers as witnesses."

He stopped flicking her clit and ignored her whimper. When her breaths had slowed a touch he growled into her ear.

"Choose."

Chapter 33

The view from the point of no return is spectacular!

Tari's whole body hummed needing release so badly it actually hurt. Dragon was pressed up against her back, strong and so damn honorable that he was letting her choose. She looked to the left and realized that even tucked back behind this tall table they had an audience.

Most people were partying or caught up in their own conversations. The music was loud, but if Dragon fucked her right here, people would hear her screams of pleasure.

Already a few Brothers and people she didn't know were watching, as he played with her as she leaned on the table. A scream of pleasure came from Pixie and Tari's body tightened in response. She wanted Dragon to claim her for everyone here to know he was hers.

Trying to catch her breath she moaned, "*Te necesito,* Dragon. Claim me."

His hand started working her clit again and the orgasm

that had backed off rushed over her. She clutched at the sides of the table not wanting to lose her balance. Pleasure ricocheted inside her and a load moan escaped her lips.

"You going to make my fantasies come true, *Mami*? I get to fuck you standing up, those long legs and perfect ass pressed against me."

"Yes, please. I need you inside me."

She felt Dragon raise her skirt then the warm length of him sliding against her folds. The room and the people watching meant nothing. She wanted him to thrust quickly and fill her up, but instead he slowly entered her. Each and every inch of him rubbing against her walls in sensuous torture.

Tari tried to buck against him but his strong hands held her still. When he was fully seated inside her, his hand reached around and started slow circles over her sensitized clit.

"You're going to come like this for me, *Mami* so I can feel your greedy pussy pulling me in. Then I'm going to fuck you so hard there will be no doubt to anyone here that you're mine." His hand moved from her clit around to her ass. His voice dropped lower sending chills down her spine. "One day I'm going to claim this ass, and you're going to beg me to do it."

He started a slow glide that lit all her nerves on fire. His fingers circling her clit with slowly increasing speed. The music and sounds of the people around her slowly faded and felt like their bodies were merging in a slow primal beat. Her hands shook with the effort it took to just stand still and not demand more. He shifted his hips and it was like the world exploded in light as he rubbed against a magic place inside her. This orgasm didn't break, it just kept going. Dragon picked up speed and she tossed her head trying to absorb what he was doing to her.

"You're mine, *reina*, my Old Lady."

"God, yes. I'm yours, only yours."

His hips thrust forward slamming into her and finally the wave broke the orgasm blinding her for a moment. His body owned every inch of hers, the slap of his hips against her like a heartbeat against her soul as she let go and flew. His own shout of completion was loud, and she felt it deep in her bones.

"Dark Sons for life!" Dragon's hoarse voice called out loudly.

"Dark Sons for life!" Was echoed around the room.

Tari's cheeks heated as Dragon carried her over to a couch near the front door. Her legs had given out and she wasn't sure if they would ever work again. All the walking today, and then the orgasms, had her still healing body ready to go on strike.

"You okay, *mi reina*?" Dragon ran a concerned hand down her cheek.

She smiled, loving he was worried. "I'm fine, it was just a long energetic day. My body is not quite up to speed yet."

"You make me forget all sense. Can I get you something?" The concern in his voice made her feel special.

"I have to clean up, but first I would love some juice." Tari gave him what she hoped wasn't a tired smile. What she really wanted to do was curl up and go to sleep but knew he would have to stay for a while longer.

"I think I can do that. You wait here." He kissed her forehead and walked toward the bar.

Tari chuckled as she saw him getting back slaps and congratulations as he worked his way through the crowd. It was embarrassing in a way that made her feel special. She was now officially part of this odd family. A stranger with greasy blond hair squatted in front of her, blocking her view. Tari jerked back into the chair trying to put some distance between her and this rude man.

"Say anything, make any fuss, and your daughter dies." His voice was like gravel but his words hit her like a splash of cold water.

The man held up his phone on it was a picture of Mama Rios with a black eye and bloodied lip clutching Citlali to her chest. Bile burned up her throat as adrenaline raced through her body. They were still wearing the same clothes they had been when she last saw them.

"What do you want?" Tari's voice trembled with fear and rage.

The man swiped over to the call screen and hit dial before handing her the phone. She took it with shaking fingers and placing it against her ear.

The ringing stopped and a male voice came over the line.

"Nefertari Johnson, I want you to listen very closely."

Tari recognized his voice and Californian accent as the officer from the hospital who had threatened her. But now that she had her memories back, a second older memory made her want to sob. He had been at Dark Zen and yelled at her when she had tried to talk to the young girl walking him back for a private session. The Ukrainian girl much too young to be working as a massage therapist. The incident that had almost gotten her fired for speaking anything other than English around the customers. Tari looked around hoping someone was paying attention but the party was in full swing and the bodies of strangers blocked out the sight of anyone who might help her.

"Officer Volker?" Pieces fell into place. Master V, the young girl, Dark Zen, all of it was connected to this man.

"I said listen!" Tari flinched at the rage in his voice. "If you want your little girl alive, you're going to walk calmly out with my man and get into his car. In ten minutes, if I don't hear from him, your daughter and the old lady die."

Tari breathed deep trying to find calm in the chaos swirling in her brain. What should she do or say? Before she could decide a click sounded and the call ended. Going wasn't smart but if there was any chance Volker would keep his word it was worth any risk on her part.

The man in front of her took her arm in a painful grip and pulled her out of the chair. Numbly she stumbled next to him, tears blinding her as she put one foot in front of the other. Would people notice and try and stop them? She tilted her head down to try and hide the tears she couldn't stop. They were out the front door and walking towards the parking lot, gravel under her boots making walking hard, when the music inside the Clubhouse cut off.

The few people outside turned to look toward the building in confusion. Her kidnapper picked up his pace and when they reached a beat-up sedan practically threw her down on the back seat. Covering his actions with his own body he cuffed her hands behind her. He pulled a black hood over her head and everything went dark. For her daughter she had to stay still. She couldn't risk fighting.

Tari heard Hawk's distant voice cut through the night. "Party's over, everyone out! Brothers, lock this place down."

Fear and hope fought for supremacy in Tari's heart. Had they realized she was missing? If they stopped her Volker would kill her daughter. The cotton of the hood absorbed her tears as she heard the car door slam. The vibration of the car through the seats matched the shivering of her muscles as she fought back sobs.

She counted as she felt movement, trying to find some sort of peace in the darkness that was her reality now.

"I got the girl and we're heading your way." Tari strained to hear anything praying that Volker had kept his word. "No one is following but there was some sort of dust up right as we left… Will do."

She hadn't prayed in a long time but found herself doing so now. Lost in darkness, without much hope, she didn't know if she was praying to God, the Universe, or Dragon but she hoped one of them would hear and answer.

"When I am afraid, I will trust in you. I will not be afraid. What can mortal man do to me?" She whispered the barely remembered bible quote under her breath, her jaw clenched. Not caring if it was the Christian thing to do, she added, "Lord, if I can't save my daughter let her father's wrath be slow, painful, and lacking all mercy."

Chapter 34

Too little too late ?

Dragon pushed his way through the crowd, accepting the teasing congratulations from Brothers and strangers alike. Tari looked beat and after getting her a drink he fully intended on taking her back to his place to rest. With how sexy she had looked he had completely forgotten she was still recovering. He pushed in next to Ink and Hannibal at the bar annoyed at himself for not taking her back there immediately.

"Saw you pinned your filly down. Guess she won't be peeping at our door tonight." Ink's Texas drawl somehow cut through the noise without shouting.

Dragon laughed. "Not tonight at least."

Hannibal raised an eyebrow. "Didn't think you shared."

"Oh, I don't. My girl likes to watch and I love how hot that makes her."

Ink slapped him on the shoulder. "Always glad to help out a Brother."

Just past the bar Hawk strode out of the back hallway his face grim. When a hanger on didn't move fast enough the president knocked him aside.

"Something's up." Dragon pointed across the room and they watched as Hawk ripped the cord to the sound system out of the wall.

Dragon pushed away from the bar and started walking in that direction with his two Brothers at his back.

"Party's over. Brothers, we're on lockdown."

Fuck. He had to get Tari safe and make sure everyone cleared out. Hawk's gaze caught his own and Dragon's stomach dropped as the man gestured for him to follow.

He looked around the room trying to see if Tari was okay but the mass of people now being pushed out the door by Brothers and prospects hid that side of the room.

"We'll get your girl secured. You go to Hawk." Hannibal's words loosened something inside him.

He nodded. "Thanks, Brother. She is on the couch by the front door."

Dragon pushed through the crowd following his President down the hall into his office. Highdive and Max were already in the room looking grim.

"One minute and I'll brief you. Where's your girl?" Hawk's serious tone had Dragon's blood pumping.

"Hannibal and Ink are securing her."

Hawk nodded and the office door swung open as Sharp and Dozer entered the room. All the Officers were here except Tek, the fact he was being included didn't mean anything good.

Hawk hit a button on his desk phone and spoke, "Everyone's here."

Tek's voice came out of the speaker. "To catch you all up,

we have people who monitor police calls near any address of interest to us. Two hours ago a possible carjacking was reported two miles from Mama Rios' house." Dragon's heart froze as what that could mean hit him. "Police investigated and reported it was a prank call. As a security measure we sent men out to do a safety check as a precaution. They didn't find her at home but didn't see any signs of violence. It took some time but we tracked her phone and found it on the side of the road with her purse which had blood on it."

The floor felt like it dropped out from under him. His mother was out there somewhere possibly hurt or worse. "She had my daughter with her!" His throat constricted. "Did you find her car?"

Thank God, the Dark Sons had their own special type of LoJack on every one of their families' vehicles.

"It was abandoned a few miles away in a parking lot." Tek's voice told him there was no good news to follow.

Dragon felt the overwhelming need to punch something. "*Mierda!*"

Hawk leaned forward. "Every Brother is going to hit the streets none of us will stop until we find them."

Dragon growled. "It's fucking Volker it has to–" The door flung open.

Ink rushed in, panting. "Tari's gone. We have Brothers checking every car as it leaves but Grinder said he saw Flak running for his bike right as the lockdown was called and taking off like he was chasing someone."

Dragon had to grip the edge of the desk to keep himself upright. His whole world was crumbling right in front of him right in the moment it had finally been perfect. His Brothers wisely gave him space and silence while he processed.

"I'll start tracking Flak and Tari's phones and call you back when I have something." Tek's voice was immediately followed by a disconnect.

Dragon slammed his fists on the desk causing everything to shake. His scream of primal rage causing all the men around him to tense. He wanted to smash everything around him. Make the chaos swirling in his mind a physical reality.

Focusing on his breathing he pulled himself under control. Destroying this room would do nothing to bring them back. He looked up and searched the eyes of these men, the Officers of his new family and knew there was nothing they wouldn't do to bring his women home. They were his Brothers; he would lay down his life for them as they would do for him.

Hawk nodded. "Highdive and Ink, get the gear and weapons ready. I want every Brother ready to ride as soon as we have a location. Sharp and Dozer check on lockdown I want all families accounted for and secure. Max you organize who rides together and prepare team plans if we need to split up."

Each man touched his shoulder as they quickly moved out of the room to follow Hawk's orders.

"I'm not going to give you any pussy platitudes, Brother. We will find him. He's not smart enough, nor is this earth big enough, for him to hide from us. Go get geared up and put your head on straight. Your women need you at your best."

Dragon barely registered the time it took to get ready, his training allowing him to check and ready the weapons laid out for him. The bone conduction earpieces and throat mics on every man, along with the quiet professional way his Brothers prepared, let him know they all took this as seriously as he did.

"Listen up!" Hawk's bellow had every man's attention. "We received a text from Flak. He saw Tari and is in pursuit. We've told him to hang back unless she is in immediate danger."

It was the right move, Dragon knew it, but he wanted his woman safe now. He sent out a prayer that she would hold on.

"Tek will coordinate tactical once we have a final location. Get with your Road Captains. We're moving out." Hawk made a rounding up gesture and they all started moving towards bikes and vans.

Max stood in front of Dragon, his face serious. "You're riding with me, Hawk, Sharp and Highdive. Your comms are on the Officer channel so you'll know what we know. Can we count on you to keep your head?"

Dragon didn't think he could talk so he nodded. He'd been on countless missions for the SEALs, never once had he doubted his training, but this was personal and he knew his own instincts would get in the way. He had to trust in the men, his Brothers, to see him and his family safely through the other side.

"Good. Tek has done some magic so he can use Flak's phone as a microphone. Once it starts giving any good info he'll patch it through." Max gave him a quick look up and down. "Let's go get them back."

Chapter 35

Mess with me and I'll let Karma do its job. Mess with my child and I become Karma.

Tari felt the car finally park and tried to prepare herself for what was to follow. Why this lunatic had focused on her, still confused her. She hadn't done anything to him except survive and try to find happiness for her and her daughter. She hadn't even told the cops what she had remembered yet.

The door opened and rough hands tore her out of the car, dumping her onto the dirt. The hood fell off and she blinked trying to get her eyes to focus. Rocks and twigs dug into her palms as she looked up at what appeared to be an expensive forest retreat. At least five vehicles were parked in front of the large building. Only the front porch lights illuminated the yard, leaving the surrounding area in deep shadows.

"Get up you stupid bitch!" The impact of her kidnapper's

kick pushed her forward and she scrambled unsteadily to her feet.

Adrenaline and exhaustion twisted within her as she was roughly escorted inside. The lodge-like house felt too upscale for what was going on. Nice furnishings were contrasted by the armed thugs in worn clothing. Two figures were sitting on an oversized leather couch. Energy flooded her system as she ran towards Mama Rios. The woman had a protective arm around Citlali who lay curled up, asleep against her side.

Not wanting to wake the little girl, Tari dropped to her knees soaking in the sight of her daughter. She had to bite back a scream as she noticed the swelling and split lip on the left side of her little angel's face.

"That *Pendejo* officer hit her when she wouldn't stop crying." Mama Rios also looked battered and a little bloody. Her right eye and lip were swollen and flecks of dried blood were visible on her clothes and skin. Hot tears of rage burned down Tari's face.

Volker stormed into the room looking disheveled and agitated. The man had the nerve to still be wearing his badge on his belt while committing crimes. Tari wanted more than anything to claw this man's eyes out but knew one of the five other men in the room would stop her and what would that accomplish?

"*Por Que?*" Tari's choice was choked with emotion as stress caused her to struggle with her words. "Why? Why me? What could you possibly want?"

Volker grabbed Tari by the hair and dragged her to her feet. In her heels she was taller than the detective which caused her to have to bend forward in his grip to keep her hair from being pulled out. He threw her backwards causing her to trip over a coffee table and sprawl on the ground.

Lali woke at the noise and began to cry. "Mama!"

Mama Rios held her granddaughter tightly trying to give comfort and quiet her.

"Why?" Volker gave an almost manic laugh. "You are the only witness who can tie me to Dark Zen. If you would have just died like you were supposed to, none of this," he gestured to the couch, "would have been necessary."

"*Fine,* kill me. *Just let* them go," Tari pleaded.

Volker sneered at her. "Of course, I'm going to kill you. And them. Only choice you have is if they suffer before they die."

Citlali's cries were muffled by Mama Rios' chest. The older woman looked so proud as if unafraid of the fate just described. Tari scanned the faces of the men in the room. Some appeared uncomfortable, but none gave any indication they would do anything to stop what was going on.

"My daughter is una *bebe*. She is no danger to you, *ella* can barely talk." Tari pleaded with the monster now looming over her. Her words felt jumbled, but she prayed he would see reason.

"Tell you what, I'll have my men lock her in the bathroom. You do what I say, tell me what I want to know, and we leave her there, untouched. Maybe someone finds her before she starves, maybe not."

Tari knew it was the best and only deal she would be getting. It tore at her heart that Mama Rios was going to die with her, but she doubted these men would be leaving any witnesses.

The man who had kidnapped her snatched a screaming Lali out of her grandmother's arms and vanished with the thrashing child.

"Mommy! No! Want Mommy!" A minute later the cries were muffled by a closed door and Tari's heart broke as she heard Lali's little fists hitting a door.

When the man who had carried away her daughter reentered the room, Volker smirked. "I'm going to ask you some questions, and for each you don't answer, Michael is going to hurt the old woman."

Tari nodded, not knowing what this insane man could possibly want to know.

"Your stunt with telling the Dark Sons about my little side business has caused me problems. I was just a few months away from retiring, now I have the Cartel breathing down my neck for their drugs, and the Russians wanting their money. Tell me where your boyfriend's gang hid the drugs and girls."

Tari was stunned. Why would this maniac think she would know anything that could be helpful? If she told him the truth, he would harm Dragon's mother. Michael pulled out his gun and pointed it at Mama Rios.

"*They have a vault in the basement of their club.*" Tari made up the only lie she could think of.

"Speak English you stupid whore!" Volker snarled.

Her heart raced but no matter how hard she tried, the words went fuzzy in her mind and she knew nothing she said was in English.

"Shoot the woman in the leg."

"*No!*" Tari scrambled up trying to stop the gunshot that echoed through the room.

She threw herself at the woman who had called her daughter, covering the woman's body with her own. More gunshots echoed and Tari braced herself, waiting for pain and the death that would follow.

"*Mija*, are you okay?" Tari looked down into the concerned eyes of Mama Rios unable to believe they both seemed to be okay.

Pain lanced through her scalp as she was ripped off of the couch by her hair. Mama Rios' shocked expression was replaced with Michael's lifeless eyes staring at her from the floor. Volker dragged her across the room as she scrambled trying to find footing. She was tossed down on a blood covered body.

The olive complexion and handsome sharp features drew memories of a laughing man trying to tease her into a smile. He had guarded her in the hospital and tried to calm her when she had a panic attack at the Clubhouse. The prospect who had been so friendly was lying next to her. Unseeing eyes let her know that his last act on this earth had been to step between a bullet and her.

"Who is that?" Volker snarled.

"*Flak. His name was Flak.*" Tari sent up a prayer for the soul of the man who had tried to save them.

"How the fuck did he find us?"

Tari gave Volker an incredulous look. Like his earlier questions, she was baffled as to why he thought she could answer.

"I hope we're interrupting." The voice that came from the direction of the front door was completely unfamiliar and heavily accented. If Tari had to guess the man was from southern Russia near the Kazakhstan border.

Volker moved, revealing five new men, four with weapons out and pointed at the people in the room. They held their weapons with steady hands, their looks daring any of the men in the room to move without permission. Distinctive black-work tattoos peeked out of the collars of their black t-shirts and Tari was left with no doubt that these were the Russians Volker had spoken of earlier. The Bratva, or Russian Mafia, were easy to pick out with their tattoos – a roadmap of their lives. A random Russian bad guy would have been bad enough, but from what little she knew from living in Eastern Europe, these men would be smart and ruthless.

"Andrey. What are you doing here?" Volker postured puffing up like he wasn't the one at gunpoint.

"I think maybe you should call me Mr. Petrov." The man not holding a gun spoke.

"Fine." The word was ground out between clenched teeth. "Mr. Petrov what are you doing here?"

Petrov walked forward, his men falling in behind him with their weapons still drawn. "You don't return my calls. You are not at your home or work. The houses where my girls are supposed to be, are empty. I am thinking you are trying to fuck me."

"They aren't your girls, they're mine," Volker growled. Tari couldn't believe he was acting so hostile in the face of so many guns.

One of the over-muscled goons adjusted his aim to point directly at the dirty cop. "*Should I kill him?*" he asked in Russian.

"*Not yet. I may still be able to squeeze some money out of him before we kill him.*" Petrov switched back to English. "You have not finished paying for them and your payment is late."

"I'm not one of your flunkies to be ordered around. You'll get your money. I'm just cleaning up some internal matters."

Tari got a crazy idea, and before she could think better, she spoke softly in Russian. "*He lies like an American politician. He will be burning in hell by daybreak and you will never see a cent.*"

Volker kicked her in the ribs and she curled into a ball to protect herself. When no second blow landed, she looked up to see Volker being held at gunpoint while Petrov made disappointed clicking sounds.

"The bitch is just one of my whores. She barely speaks English, only Spanish." Volker held still but his whole body trembled.

"That did not sound like Spanish to me." Petrov switched to Russian. "*Is what he said true, midnight flower? Are you one of his whores?*"

Tari stood up doing her best to ignore the dead man at her feet. She pulled back her shoulders and looked Petrov in the eyes for a moment before dropping her gaze as his culture preferred. "*I am no man's whore.*"

The Russian looked her up and down. "*You dress like a putana.*"

"*I was dressed for my man before this piece of shit kidnapped me.*"

"What the fuck is she saying?" Volker's face was red, his eyes wild.

Tari noticed Citlali's yelling had finally stopped. She hoped her little girl had calmed. She sent up a prayer her daughter would be forgotten in all this chaos.

Mama Rios was sitting thin lipped on the couch and Volker's men looked on the verge of running away. The three still alive bunched up near the back sliding-glass door as if they intended to bolt.

"She says you are lying to me."

"Fucking bitch!" Volker stepped forward but was pulled up short when Tari saw Petrov tap his forehead with the muzzle of a gun.

Tari drew on every bit of courage she had and decided on an all or nothing bluff. She drew herself up to her full height and put the queen, Dragon had named her, into her voice. "*He has started a war with the Dark Sons. The man dead at my feet is a Dark Son, I am the Old Lady of a Dark Son, she is the mother of a Dark Son, and the child screaming in the other room is the daughter of a Dark Son. If you let this man kill us you will be at war. I promise you, you don't want to fuck with the Dark Sons.*"

Petrov's lip twitched upward in an almost smile. "*I like a strong woman. But you forget, little sun, no one knows I am here. This man owes me one hundred thousand dollars. Are you worth that to your man?*"

Tari held her facade not sure what to do. She had no idea if the Dark Sons would pay to get her back. She looked over at Mama Rios hoping for some inspiration. There had to be something she could promise this man.

"Pity." Petrov looked back at Volker. "Do you have my money?"

"Yes." Tari wondered if the detective was lying. "It's in the safe in the bedroom down that hall."

"You had better not be lying to me."

Terror rose up inside of Tari like a wave. If Volker did have the money what would that mean for her and Mama Rios? Shadows danced outside the front window drawing her attention. Was someone out there?

Chapter 36

Winning can be bittersweet ?

"P*ackage secure*." Dozer's deep voice whispered across their comms.

Though he couldn't see them, Dragon knew his daughter was in Dozer's arms. She would be safe. The throbbing of his pulse against his throat lessoned. The sound of the gunshots as they came over the line via Flak's cell had almost broken him. He couldn't dwell on it now, but he owed his sanity and future happiness to that man's sacrifice.

The cool night was starting to seep into his bones as they stood outside waiting for the signal to breach. The only thing keeping him still was he could hear Tari's voice through the coms. He couldn't understand most of what she said, as she was speaking mostly in Russian, but her voice kept him level.

Hawk chuckled low and Dragon glared at him. The four of them were crouched next to the front door ready to make entry once the snipers called the ready.

"Your woman just threatened a high-ranking member of the Russian Mafia. Apparently if the Bratva don't man up and protect her, they will be at war with the Dark Sons." Hawk's whispered words had them all smiling.

Dragon shook his head in wonder. Tari had a heart of gold, the soul of a saint, and a backbone made of titanium. She was more than he ever dreamed he could have and never again would he let her be in this level of danger.

"In position. Three ducks lined up right in a row." Sharp's status was the last piece to be put into play.

Dragon watched Hawk key on his mic. "O*n my signal take down ducks. All teams, hard entry. Only engage Russians if necessary. If possible, take primary dickhead alive."*

Several clicks could be heard over the line confirming the orders. Highdive stood up pressing against the side of the door ready to open it for the rest of the team to enter.

"In 5..4..3..2"

Glass shattered on the silent count of one. Highdive threw open the door and Dragon charged in with Hawk and the rest of his team at his back. Two men lay dead off to the right and a third off to the left on the floor near his mother. He was proud she had crouched down behind a couch arm taking cover and out of any line of fire. Near the back of the room four men in business suits protected a fifth.

Grinder raced from the back picking up Mama under his arm. With Colt covering him, they quickly made an exit. Tari stood like the Egyptian queen she had been named after staring down the barrel of a gun held by Volker. The Russians had retreated to a corner, their guns out but smartly not pointed at any of the fifteen, well-armed, and pissed off Dark Sons.

Hawk slung his AR around to his back. "Drop the gun, Volker."

"I drop the gun and you kill me." Volker's hands were

shaking but he kept the gun up and pointed at the woman Dragon loved.

The man wasn't wrong, and it put them all in an impossible position.

"*I don't have a shot.*" Sharp's frustrated voice came over the comms.

At this range, every man here could take out the fucker, but it would take a surprise shot at the base of his skull to insure he couldn't also pull the trigger.

Volker was positioned a few feet away from a closed closet door with Tari between him and most of the room. Hawk and Dragon were closest to Tari on the right, Max and Ink were closest to Volker to the left. No way to get anyone behind him.

"*Bud' gotov.*" Dragon winced at how Tari's voice trembled despite her calm appearance. Her language problems obviously flaring under stress.

"Speak English!" Volker screamed, but it didn't seem to bother his woman.

She looked to the right and her eyes went wide. Her face filled with terror as she looked over Volker's shoulder. "No. Don't, he'll shoot me!"

Dragon stood shocked as he watched Volker spin to face an invisible enemy. Tari practically dove into his arms as Max tackled the now off-balance idiot. Dragon gripped his woman and spun them so his body shielded hers.

"Clear," Max called out.

Everyone was silent for several long seconds before Ink's Texas twang rolled through the room. "Did she use, 'Oh my God, look over there!' and it worked?"

Masculine laughter filled the room and Dragon held his woman tight. He looked at her beautiful face and was amazed at the small smile on her lips.

"You found me."

"I would find you anywhere, *mi reina*."

"Citlali is in a room somewhere." Tari looked around.

"Dozer got her out before we ever came in." Dragon brushed a quick kiss across his woman's lips before looking toward the man who had created so much pain.

Volker stood with his hands zip-tied behind his back, Max holding him in place.

Dragon nodded thanks to his Brother. "Good reflexes."

Max snorted. "Your woman told me to be ready. Though I had no idea for what."

Dragon looked over at Tari who just shrugged.

"Fuck you all." Volker's spit barely missed him.

Tari surprised Dragon by striding up and punching Volker straight in the dick. The man crumpled to his knees and she kicked him in the face, stumbling back from the force of her kick. "That is for hitting my baby girl."

Dragon's growl was echoed by several of his Brothers. "He hit Citlali?"

Rage had his muscles chording with tension as Tari nodded.

"She's out in the van with Mama, you should go out to them." His voice was flat, his eyes locked on the man who would soon have his undivided attention.

Tari started walking towards the door, then paused, and in a quiet voice said, "For every nightmare our little girl is going to have, he should pay in pain. Be an instrument of Karma." Her words stunned him. She reached up and kissed him before striding out the door into the night.

"You must be quite a man to tame one such as her." The Russian's voice drew Dragon's attention back to the fact things were not done.

Hawk stepped forward crossing his arms over his chest. "Andrey Petrov."

"Jonathan Windsor." Petrov raised an eyebrow. Dragon was shocked. He had known Hawk's given name was John but not his last name. How did this guy?

"When did you expand from drugs and overpriced loans to peddling underage girls?"

"Phftt." Petrov waved a hand. "This I did not do. Officer Volker borrowed the money to start his business from me. The girls were his collateral."

"You're walking a fine line with our agreement." Hawk's voice was deeper than usual.

"Ah, but I am on the right side of that line. I do not traffic in women, do not sell my product to your people, or on your property. You and your men do not bother me or mine."

Dragon knew the Dark Sons had treaties with many underground organizations, he just hadn't realized the Bratva was one of them. Deals like this were what kept them safe and let them hold their territories and protect their families, but it didn't mean he had to like it.

"You going to have a problem with this?" Hawk nodded to the bound man groaning on the floor.

"I get my money, my business is done." The Russian shrugged.

"And the collateral?" Hawk's voice dripped with disgust.

"If the debt is paid the collateral is of no interest to me."

"You'll have your money tomorrow."

The two men nodded and the Russians put away their weapons. It turned Dragon's stomach that bottom feeders like that could walk away without consequence. He studied his President's face but, as usual, there were no clues to be had there.

Crash slung his rifle to his back. "Smoke and I will look for the safe he said held the money."

Even if the money wasn't found, Dragon had a feeling the

Club would be covering the cost to ensure the freedom of the girls Volker had abused for God only knew how long. He squatted down next to Volker and pulled the whimpering man's face up by his hair.

"You and me. We're going to spend some time together."

Chapter 37

Fighting makes me hotter than a leather seat in August.

Tari woke to Dragon's warm arms lifting her out of her daughter's bed. A quick glance down showed her little angel snuggled fast asleep in a pile of stuffed animals. She wrapped her arms around his neck and settled her head against his chest, soaking in the steady rhythm of his heart. The first rays of morning sunshine peeped around the curtains, giving an almost mystical feel to the apartment.

She didn't want to ruin this time together with questions about the previous night, but she needed to know one thing. "Is it over?"

"Yes. *Mi reina.*" He laid her down on the large, soft bed that she had yet to sleep in. Long, damp, black hair framed his chiseled features. He wasn't wearing a shirt and her eyes couldn't help but wander his sculptured tattooed arms and chest. Black sweats hung low on his hips making her wet at the promise of what was under the fabric.

She gasped as he grabbed and yanked off her sleep shorts then her tank top. His dark eyes almost glowed in the dim light. He claimed her mouth in a kiss that was somehow gentle while completely owning her.

He pressed his forehead to hers, his words a growl against her lips. "I need you, Tari. I need to breathe you in and know you are all mine."

"I'm yours. Everything I am, and everything I will be, is yours." She grabbed his chin and waited for his gaze to meet hers. "You are mine."

"Fuck. I love you, my queen." His kiss crushed her.

His hands pulled her close, their bodies skin to skin. It was as if their souls were touching, heat and desire making them one in that moment.

Dragon lifted her up and she felt him removing his pants. It only took a moment before he was inside her, filling her in the best possible way. Pleasure rolled over her as he slid against the spot deep within her; building to the ecstasy they both needed.

The danger of the evening and fear of what could have happened, had Tari on an emotional edge. She needed this as badly as he did. Needed the feeling of being alive and part of this man who had become her everything.

Her body tightened around him and fire licked up her spine. Over and over his cock rubbed against the spot deep inside that short-circuited thought and sent pleasure boiling through her. He swallowed her scream with a kiss that connected them on a spiritual level as her orgasm ripped through her.

Unbelievably, she felt a second wave coming, his thrusts pushing her higher as he slammed into the very core of her. She closed her eyes and felt as his fingers swirled on her clit causing lightning to explode behind her closed lids. Tremors of bliss set every nerve alight. For what seemed like an eternity, her mind blanked as if consumed by white fire.

Tari whimpered as she felt him pull out of her. She suddenly hated the emptiness and missed the heat of his kiss. Strong hands rolled her over to her stomach and pulled her up to her hands and knees like she was a doll. Tari looked back at Dragon over her shoulder and caught her breath at the primal vision.

He looked like an ancient warrior ready to claim his prize. His hands ran down her sweat soaked skin as if marking every part of her as his own. The pleasure that had started to fade began building again with every caress of his fingers.

"So beautiful." Dragon's hands skimmed over her ass. "I want all of you tonight, *mi reina.*"

His fingers slid through her soaking folds and up to that most forbidden of holes. He circled the delicate skin and she shivered in both fear and excitement.

"Have you ever had a man here before, *Mami?*" Dragon's finger pressed barely inside her causing strange zips of sensation.

"No." Tari gasped, not sure if she enjoyed the sensations the new nerves caused.

His other hand found her clit and began slow swirls as he moved in and out going deeper and stretching her just a bit. The two sensations had her mind whirling. She knew she shouldn't enjoy him finger fucking her ass but the evidence was quickly growing that she might.

He leaned over her, opening the drawer in the nightstand. The snick of a cap was followed by cool liquid dripping down the crack of her ass. He rubbed the silky oil around her rosette, and she whimpered when two fingers started stretching her open.

It was like a war between her sensations and her mind. It hurt a little but, more, it was strange and exhilaratingly dirty.

"You going to give this to me? Let me have every part of you?" His fingers started a slow scissoring motion that pulsed. His fingers on her clit picked up speed causing her breath to shorten into gasps.

"Uhm… Ah… Sure." Her voice was barely a whisper. Unsure she did want it but not wanting to deny him anything.

The sharp pain on her ass-cheek caused her to glare over her shoulder to see Dragon's almost feral gaze.

"You bit me!"

He nipped her ass again at the same time his fingers slapped hard against her clit. It was both pain and pleasure in a confusing way. He started slowly, pinching the bundle of nerves in front while twisting his fingers inside her.

"Sure, is not an answer. I want you to beg me to fuck your ass, *Mami*. Tell me you are mine and you want my cock deep inside that virgin ass."

Her pussy gushed at his words and she pushed back against his fingers wanting to feel filled. His fingers on her clit began rubbing at a faster tempo and she felt her orgasm rising. Right as she would have crashed over the edge his hands stopped.

"Say it!" Dragon growled.

Tari bared her teeth, something primal coming over her. "Make me."

Dragon's eyes lit up with the challenge. He played her body like a master bringing her right to the edge of orgasm over and over but not letting her fall over. On the fifth repetition sweat soaked her skin and every muscle trembled with the need to come.

"Say it," Dragon growled in her ear.

"Fuck me, Dragon! Fuck my ass!"

His fingers flew over her clit as she felt his thick length slowly sliding into her ass inch by inch. It was overwhelming and wonderful. The orgasm that ripped through her was more than just physical, her heart and spirit flew outward and shattered in glorious harmony.

"Come on my cock. Fuck yes, *mi reina.*"

It was like a damn broke and they were wild beasts primal and unhinged. He slammed into her, his grunts matching hers. The slap of their skin, an ancient heartbeat filling the room.

His roar of satisfaction and the warm jets of his cum triggered another small orgasm. The two of them collapsed forward on the bed, their breaths mingling. Tari felt his heartbeat against her skin and knew no matter what the future held they could face it together.

"*Te amo, Gabor.*"

"*Te amo, Nefertari.*"

The sound of a door opening down the hall and running little footsteps had both of them chuckling.

Epilogue

I t was Friday afternoon, two weeks after Flak's funeral and Dozer had invited some of the Brothers over for an impromptu barbeque before the usual wild times at the Clubhouse. Watching the Brothers as they mourned the loss of Flak had been heartbreaking. Mama Rios honored the memory of the man who had saved them by burning a candle for him every Sunday at church. The love, dedication, and loyalty that had led him to sacrifice himself would never be forgotten. Tari was determined to live every day to the fullest so she repaid that gift in some small way.

Tari watched Citlali with joy as she giggled and played in the blow-up bounce house with the other Dark Sons' children. Three weeks had passed since the kidnapping and her little girl was flourishing in this newfound family. She was too. Physical therapy and daily yoga had done wonders and she was almost back to normal. Mama Rios visited often and had become dearer to her heart than her own adoptive mother had ever been.

"The sound of children's laughter is the song of Angels on earth." Val's warm southern drawl made her turn, smiling.

The warmth of Dragon's arm around her waist was a wonderful addition to the perfect afternoon. Dozer had his arm around her wild and wonderful friend as they walked up.

"That it is." Tari gave Val a hug while Dragon and Dozer stuck to manly chin lifts.

"So Queenie." Val winked. "You going to have another?"

Tari laughed, shaking her head. While Dragon had given her the road name *Reina* everyone else had picked the playful translation after what they called her royal decrees for vengeance.

"I want to finish my physical therapy degree, plus we're saving up to build a house here on the compound. We should probably wait." Tari would like nothing better than to have more children with Dragon but was determined to do it right this time.

"Think we can help out there." Dozer gave his woman a smile.

Val was practically bouncing with what looked like excitement and Tari gave her a puzzled look.

"We're building y'all a house next to ours!" Val squealed. Tari was shocked and looked over at Dragon who looked equally as stunned.

"Appreciated, Brother but not necessary." Dragon seemed to struggle with what to say as he looked at Dozer.

"Don't you let pride come before your fall as I knock you down." Val gave a stern look at them both. "This is my gift to Tari and there is going to be no arguments."

Tari's throat tightened. She wanted a home for her and Dragon but this was way too much. "Val. I–"

"Zip it, girl." Val's smile went soft and she leaned a little against Dozer her hand coming up to rest on her stomach. "I told you before you were a light in my darkest times. You helped me find my way back and now I want to say thank you."

Tears of hope shimmered Tari's vision. "Val, are you…?"

The southern woman smiled and nodded. Tari let joy wash over her and she pulled her friend into a laughing hug.

"I'm so happy for you!"

"Besides, I need you to get started on making my baby another playmate. With Pixie's child, we can have the three amigos."

The two Brothers gave each other back slaps and Tari looked around. "Where is Pixie?"

"She is over getting the dirt on the woman Tek brought with him."

Tari scanned the crowd of Brothers and their families. "Tek has a woman?"

"Seems so and she is not his usual filly."

Tari saw Sharp and Tek talking over by the barbecue. As usual, Tek's blond clean-cut hair and looks making his Dark Sons cut seem out of character. Pixie sat at a picnic table talking to a woman with vibrant purple hair.

Actually Pixie's own blonde hair and sweet style set her apart from what Tari would have pictured as a biker babe. Looking around at the men and women in the compound, made her realize all of her preconceived notions were silly. What made these people family wasn't something visible, it was the unseen Brotherhood and Sisterhood that was stronger than any blood.

"You know what, Val." Tari looked over and caught Dragon's eye. "I would love to live next to you and nothing says I can't finish school and grow our family at the same time."

Dragon's hug swept her off her feet and swung her around in a circle.

"Me too, Papa! Up!"

Tari squealed as Dragon managed to swoop their daughter into the impromptu game. His strength amazed her as he swung them in a large circle before planting a kiss on both their cheeks.

This was the moment she had dreamed of. With her hands she cupped Citlali's and Dragon's cheeks.

"*Te amo.*"

The End

Book Three - Coming Soon

Caught in the Dark - Tek's Story

Ann Jensen

I'm a snarky Jersey Woman who dreamed of one day becoming an Author. I write Romance with bigger than life characters who have to dodge every obstacle I gleefully throw in their paths. Somehow my characters also find time for steamy fun on their way to their HEAs.

I'm an avid reader, engineer, photographer, and a proud Bi woman. My life is a journey that I hope never stops in one place too long. I fill it with love and laughter whenever possible and when I can't, I pull out my clue by four and use it with deadly precision.

https://annjensenwrites.com/

Dark Sons Motorcycle Club
Saved by the Dark
Lost in the Dark

Blushing Books

Blushing Books is one of the oldest eBook publishers on the web. We've been running websites that publish spanking and BDSM related romance and erotica since 1999, and we have been selling eBooks since 2003. We hope you'll check out our hundreds of offerings at http://www.blushingbooks.com.

Blushing Books Newsletter

Please join the Blushing Books newsletter
to receive updates & special promotional offers.
You can also join by using your mobile phone:
Just text BLUSHING to 22828.

Made in the USA
Columbia, SC
20 September 2021

45841346R00155